THE CHRISTMAS MIRACLE BELL

EILA TRENT

To my grandchildren for bringing a second wave of joy into my life. May we always be silly, laugh together and randomly dance in the driveway.
I love you. Xoxo... G-Nana & Ama

FOREWORD

Click here to join my newsletter so I can let you know when my next book is coming out.

1

❄

*E*mily rushed around her apartment and gathered all that she'd need for the next two weeks, as she placed her suitcase, tote bag and purse by the door. She checked her reflection in the long mirror and decided she liked the rust colored, wool trouser suit Cooper bought for her. For Christmas he bought her a new wardrobe, some of which she'd wear while on vacation at his parents' house. She wondered if her choice of clothing had ever embarrassed him in the early days of their relationship.

The phone rang as she headed toward the kitchen to grab the gift she just wrapped.

"Hey, Sally, how's the all-time best sister ever?" Emily giggled as she poured coffee into her travel mug and set it by her purse.

"Hi, Em, I just wanted to call and check in with you before you left. How's it going? Are you ready to spend the next two weeks with the ultra-rich?" Sally snickered.

"Ugh, I hate going to Hamilton House and why do they need to call it that? Well, I'm packed and I think I've got everything but you know what? I'm kinda worried. Cooper's been acting a little cagey for a few days, constantly confirming that I'm going with him. I don't know, Sally, I think he might be going to propose and I'm not sure I'm ready for that kind of commitment right now. I'm just so focused on my career."

"What's the problem, Emily? Jeez, he's handsome and rich, what's to be worried about? You act like being the wife of a wealthy man would be a burden." Sally giggled.

"I'm not exactly sure, I can't put my finger on it, but he's changed this last year. He seems a little more demanding and a few times he's actually been kind of rude to me. He always apologizes and then he's surprised me with some expensive gifts. Maybe that's how it is in his world, maybe that's how his parents are. And then other times I just feel like, I don't know, like I'm not good enough. He could have any woman he wants, why me?" Emily said, with doubt in her voice.

"Well, didn't you say that this last year he started working at his dad's firm? And that in just a few years he's probably going to take over the business? Maybe that's his problem, just a little too much stress living up to his father's expectations. You know I'm sure it can't be easy taking care of all that money," Sally said and laughed.

"I guess maybe you're right, Sis, but I'm not so sure that his parents like me or even approve of me. All his previous girlfriends have been from their rich inner circle, you know, blue bloods and ancestry that traces back to the Mayflower. I've met a few of the younger women in that pack and they are all drop-dead gorgeous like they just stepped off the runway in Milan, they attended the Academy Awards, or you'll see their faces in Vogue."

"Well, if you ask me, you're better than any of those silicone snobs and maybe the family needs some new blood." Sally giggled. "I've seen the way men look at you, Em, they can't help but stare at you with your long, dark hair and killer body. And those amber eyes of yours, come on girl. You could be a model yourself, like for one of those ancient Grecian sculptors, and we have Mom's Greek genes to thank for that. Really, Em, I wish you could see how beautiful you are and more importantly, you're a really good person."

"Thanks, Sally, hope you're not expecting some money for all that flattery?" Emily laughed. "Yeah, but I don't think his mom really cares for me much. It always feels like an inquisition when I'm at his parents' house, his mom has so many questions. This weekend she'll probably even ask me for my credit score." Sally giggled, but Emily didn't. "Yeah, you know, I just don't think I'm ready. Cooper was there for me when mom and dad died, but I'm not sure I want to spend the rest of my life with him, at least not yet." Emily's voice was serious.

"Well, she's just being protective of her son and all the wealth he stands to inherit. And I can't think of any woman who wouldn't jump through a few hoops, or interviews, to marry such a Ryan Gosling look-alike and with so much beautiful money. Please, be still my beating heart." Sally giggled again. "Seriously, Em, don't underestimate yourself. You have all the goods, too, but you need to do what your heart feels is right. I just know that you deserve a man who treats you like a queen, no matter how much money he has. Do what makes you happy, okay? Promise me."

Just then Emily heard a horn honk several times and she glared at the window and rolled her eyes.

"And that's another thing, he's started honking his horn at me and you know how much I hate that. I gotta go, Sally. I'll text you when I get there. Love you bunches. Bye."

"Okay, Em, be safe. And don't agree to something just because it's expected of you. Only say yes for the right reasons. Love you, too. Bye."

❄

*E*mily did a quick scan of the room. She passed through the kitchen and rushed to the door, where she grabbed all of her bags. She closed the door behind her, hurried down the few stairs and out of the entryway. When Cooper saw Emily, he got out of the car and opened the trunk.

"Emily, why do you always leave me waiting? I told you I'd pick you up at 9 a.m. this morning, that means 9 o'clock, not 9:10. My mother has planned a special, early supper for us, I don't want to be late. Successful people are never late."

"I'm sorry, Cooper, really I am. I was talking to Sally on the phone and lost track of time, that's all. Please, forgive me."

"It just seems that more and more these days you're late, or you forget something, and when that happens it affects me and my schedule, too."

Cooper and Emily got in the car. Emily could feel her face was flushed and hot, she didn't think she deserved to be spoken to like that. It seemed these days Cooper constantly chastised her. He pulled out into traffic and they sat quietly, as he exited on to the freeway. Cooper turned on the radio just to break the silence and they had driven several miles before Cooper spoke.

He patted Emily's leg. "I'm sorry that I snapped at you, Emily. I'm just having a difficult time keeping up with all that my dad expects of me, but I shouldn't take it out on you."

Emily turned to face him and sighed. "It's okay, thanks. I was hoping this would be a chance for us to relax, in the car at least, and spend some quality time together."

"Yeah, I know I've been busy, too busy. You know I love you, though, right?" Cooper smiled and glanced at Emily.

"Yes, Cooper, I do, and I love you back." Emily gave Cooper a warm smile.

"Look under your seat, I bought you something," Cooper said and grinned.

Just then his phone rang, and he saw it was his father.

"Sorry, I need to take this call."

"I know, go ahead," Emily said. She reached under her seat and her fingers found a small package. She pulled it out and looked inside; there was a small box tied with a bow. She pulled the pink ribbon and opened the box and saw a lovely pair of diamond stud earrings. Surprised and curious, she looked at Cooper. As he listened to his father, he smiled at Emily and whispered, "Put them on."

She smiled and mouthed a 'thank you' to him and did as he asked. She got the sparkling earrings in her ears and pulled down the visor mirror to look. They were beautiful and twinkled, in a thousand directions, as the sun shined through the window. She faced Cooper again to show him, but he was in a heated conversation by that time. So, she turned to look out her window as the city and cars passed by. She knew Cooper would be on the phone for a long while and he would have other calls besides his dad.

Lost in her thoughts about the morning tiff, it occurred to Emily that she had heard Cooper's father speak to his mother that way, abrupt and terse. Is that what it would be like for her if she married Cooper? The thought made her heart sink but then her mind exploded.

"Oh no, Cooper, I forgot your mother's gift, we need to turn around. We need to turn around, please," Emily begged.

"I'll call you back in a couple minutes, okay? I need to deal with something." Cooper ended the call and turned to look at her. "Okay, Emily, what? You forgot my mother's gift back at your apartment? There's no way we can turn around. That would put us behind by over an hour and Mother doesn't like it when we're late. Besides, we just passed a sign on the road that had a snowstorm warning for tonight. We have to stay ahead of it, and we'll have just enough time to get to Hamilton House and not be late for supper."

"But I won't have a gift to give to your mother. I'll be so embarrassed." Emily's face fell.

"Don't worry about it, my mother has everything she could possibly want."

"Yes, but it's the thought that counts and I'll feel so bad when I have nothing to give her." By the look on Cooper's face Emily knew they wouldn't be going back.

"Well, I'm sure it wasn't much given your finances, but the thing my mother really likes to count is money rather than thoughts. Besides, when you get home you can always mail it to her."

And with that her request was invalidated. Emily wasn't happy and was angry at herself, and now at Cooper—again. Why did he have to make remarks that seemed to always put her in her place or dismiss her feelings?

They had driven for more than an hour and a light snow had begun to fall. Ahead Cooper saw red flares on the road and vehicles had come to a complete stop. They sat there for a few minutes before a state trooper approached and Cooper rolled down his window.

"Sorry folks, but a truck has overturned up ahead and has blocked traffic on both sides. No one was hurt but it's going to take about an hour at least to get the highway cleared."

"Officer, are there any other roads to get us to Sutton?" said Cooper.

"Well, there is, the exit is about half a mile back, but I wouldn't advise it. There's supposed to be a lot of snow coming down by the end of this evening and those side roads go over the mountains and can be pretty treacherous when there's a lot of snow on them. And I'd caution that they aren't well maintained."

"Thank you, officer," Cooper said. But when the trooper was several cars up ahead, Cooper pulled out of the line, thankful he had been on the inside lane. He abruptly turned in the opposite direction and maneuvered onto the asphalt.

"Cooper, what are you doing?" Emily asked, shocked by the sudden change.

"Well, I'll tell you what I'm not doing. I'm not going to just sit on this highway for the next hour and God knows how long," Cooper snapped.

"Why are you so angry, Cooper? We'll get there eventually, and I'd rather get there safe. You should listen to what the officer said; it could be dangerous to take the other road."

"I have a lot on my mind, Emily, and a lot to do as soon as possible. And please don't question my driving." Cooper's mood had soured.

"OK," said Emily. Rather than brood about his words, she once again retreated to her thoughts as the radio played classical piano in the background, when Cooper wasn't talking on the phone. Lately she had been more comfortable in her thoughts anyway. She looked ahead when the car slowed and turned; by now there were several inches of fresh snow on the road. She looked at the sky and realized the clouds had really thickened and for a moment she felt some anxiety creep in. She wasn't sure if it was the storm brewing or being with Cooper's parents again. It never seemed to get easier with them.

2

They had driven the side road for perhaps forty minutes, and it proved to be much more scenic than the highway. Cooper had been kept busy as he talked on his phone, so Emily stared out the window. Once upon a time the road had been the major artery through this part of the country, but now was only the road you took to get to the smaller, less frequented towns. The road was scenic but slow driving as the car climbed to a much higher elevation and Cooper managed the winding curves. She watched as the snow-covered hills and the miles of trees passed by as her mind wandered. The view made her homesick, but there was no home there anymore. Her hometown and the happy life she had known as a child were only distant memories. She moved to attend college in the city, interned summers at a prestigious law firm and was offered a position as a paralegal. By all appearances, she would be an attorney in the not-so-distant future. Cooper had come into her life two years earlier and that turned into a romantic relationship. He was the son of one of the law firm's biggest clients and being trained to one day take over his father's business, so she saw him often but from a distance.

She met Cooper one day as he had exited the elevator, bumped into her and knocked the files she carried out of her hands. She stood frozen in front of him; he was even more handsome up close. He was tall and slender with piercing, blue eyes and carefully styled, thick, light brown hair. He looked like an Adonis, a hunk in a slim-cut, Italian business suit. When he bumped into her, she felt the firmness of his body as he grabbed her to block her fall. He had been quick to apologize profusely and helped pick up the mess. She saw him in the offices several more times before he asked her out for coffee. His overwhelming confidence when he spoke to her left her breathless and almost unable to answer him. He was kind, thoughtful and funny; not at all what she'd expected. In spite of his upbringing it was his charm that had won her heart. He had a business degree and had just gotten his realtor's license with a future at his father's brokerage firm. It wasn't until they'd dated for several months, and he'd driven a common man's car, that he disclosed to her how wealthy his parents were and what a privileged upbringing he'd had. Unlike her, he'd gone to only the very best schools and as a college graduation gift he'd been given a BMW. The first year Cooper had taken her to lots of fancy restaurants, short weekend trips to exciting destinations, impromptu picnics, showered her with flowers, and made it a point to spend as much time as possible just being with her. But as time passed, he'd become less like the man she first met, and perhaps, more like his father.

The first time, actually all the times, she met with his parents she had felt uneasy and sorely out of place. Although she had gone to great lengths to improve her appearance, and choice in clothing, she never felt she measured up to his mother's standards. It wasn't that she had been overtly condescending or mean, but more of the way she looked at Emily. And the questions, she always asked her so many questions. It made her feel as though she were on the witness stand with the prosecuting attorney cross examining her—on murder charges. But Mrs. Hamilton always performed her interrogations with the sweetest of smiles. And after almost two years, Emily still called them Mr. and Mrs. Hamilton. She concluded that wealthy people were fond of formality and that made her uncomfortable. Cooper even seemed different when he was with them, more serious and proper. She realized she had never seen Cooper hug his parents and she thought that was odd. It was nothing like her childhood, where her family had been demonstrative in their affection for one another, acted silly, teased and laughed a lot. Theirs was a noisy, lively home.

Her thoughts turned to her mom and dad. She missed them both, but especially the girl talks she had with her mom. She remembered the conversation she'd had that morning with Sally, and wished she could speak to her mom to ask for her guidance. Her mom was always there, ready to listen without judgement, give her best advice, and always a hug. Sometimes she'd tell Emily that there was someone else she could talk to. "God's always there Em, he's just a breath away," she would say. Emily realized she hadn't been to church nor had even thought about God since her mom and dad died. The truth be told, she was mad at God. That had been the most difficult time in her life, although she and Sally had grown closer from the shared loss. Cooper came into her life at that time, helped to distract her and did his best to lend comfort. Life used to be so much simpler and definitely happier. She wasn't sure now that moving to the city was what she had really wanted or that being a lawyer would, in the end, make her happy. She had always wanted to leave her small hometown but now she questioned all her decisions as she gazed at the wintry wonderland. She knew in her heart the most pressing concern was that she didn't know what to do about her relationship with Cooper. She knew she loved him, but was it the love-for-life kind of love?

*A*s she sighed and looked toward the road she saw the name of a town up ahead. Parsons. It was a picturesque little snapshot of a different time in American history. The buildings reflected a way of life that no city could offer. There were a lot of small shops that bid you to come and explore. Quaint signs beckoned you with promises of treasures to be discovered. Emily would have loved to spend a leisurely day searching through each store but most of them appeared to be closed for the holidays. Christmas was little more than a week away and there were only a few people on the sidewalks. As the car slowed and passed several more stores, she spotted what she hoped would be an answer to her immediate problem. Excited, she turned to face Cooper.

"Cooper, can we stop here, please? Maybe I can find a gift for your mother."

"You're kidding, right? As it is, we've lost so much time we'll be lucky to get to my parents' house in time for dessert. I don't know why you always forget things," he scolded.

"Wait, look, someone just put the open sign in the window of that antique store. Can we stop there, please, Cooper? I'll be quick. I promise."

"Okay, but please, don't keep me waiting long; you know we're already behind schedule, way behind schedule because of you."

"I won't. I'll hurry and find something." Emily smiled and gave Cooper a quick kiss.

Cooper slowed the car and parked in front of the antique store. Emily looked up at the cherubs and read the interesting sign out loud, "Celestial Antiques."

3

As Emily entered the antique store, she passed the wreath hanging on the door and inhaled deeply. As she smelled the pine, in that moment, she felt the spirit of Christmas again. She realized she'd been so busy getting ready for Christmas she'd almost forgotten the reason for her busyness. When she closed the door, wonderful fragrances filled her nostrils, she smelled cinnamon, orange, clove, and mysterious, heavenly scents that began to melt the stress she'd felt build all morning. She recognized the wonderful smell of the Christmas tree that sat in the center of the shop. Atop the tree was a brilliant star that seemed to radiate a light like none she'd ever seen before. She was drawn to the radiance, and as she approached the tree, she heard a soft voice behind her. From across the room, she thought she could hear the ringing of a bell.

"Hello, dear, what can I help you with?"

Emily turned and saw a lovely, older woman with kind, beautiful, green eyes and warm smile walk toward her; she seemed to almost float above the wooden floor. The woman had an elegance about her that was mesmerizing. She was tall and slender with refined features and chestnut colored hair pulled back into a stylish chignon.

"That star is so amazing." Emily's amber eyes were wide and focused upward, as her voice trailed off for a moment. "Oh, excuse me. I'm going with my boyfriend to his parents' home for the holidays. I forgot his mother's gift back at my apartment in the city and it's too far to go back for it."

"Well, I'm sure you'll find something here. What is she like or what does she collect?"

"Well, I'm really not sure because she's very wealthy and probably has everything, her house is magnificent. I don't have much money and she might not even like anything old, I mean antique. But I just can't go there empty handed," Emily said, in a resigned tone.

"Let's see, maybe something small or maybe something simple, maybe both. I have a lovely little bell over here and I'm sure there's no other like it." As the clerk spoke, she slowly moved her delicate hands in synchrony with her words, as if conducting a symphony.

They walked to a curio cabinet filled with different bells of every color and shape. Below each bell was a label and Emily now was very curious. As she reached for a bright blue bell, labeled 'joy', the clerk was quick to gently stop her hand.

"Oh, not that one, dear, that's meant for someone else. Here, try this, pick it up and listen to its tone. The red crystal is quite exquisite, don't you think? This is something that she won't have, it's unique, definitely one of a kind," the clerk said with a smile and caring voice, as her graceful fingers guided Emily's hand toward the other bell.

Emily gently handled the fragile-looking bell and shook it. The sound was the softest and sweetest she'd ever heard, as her hand tingled and it felt as though her heart fluttered.

"Oh my, that's lovely, almost angelic. I feel a bit light-headed, perhaps I'm dehydrated, so I should hurry. Yes, I'll take this one. What did its label say?"

As they walked to the counter, the clerk continued to speak, "This bell was from the estate of a local widow, old Mrs. Parsons. There's a rumor it belonged to her grandmother who, as a child, brought it with her from Europe, and it was believed to have been a gift from an angel. At least that's what I've heard, but maybe that's just nonsense, you know how rumors are. None the less, those little bells have been credited with several miracles over the years, according to legend. So, how long have you and your boyfriend been together?"

Emily had forgotten her earlier question to the woman and opened her purse to pay for the bell.

"We've dated for two years now. Oh, I forgot to ask how much the bell costs?" Emily worried it would be too expensive and thought about Cooper waiting for her.

"Do you think he's the one? To marry, I mean," the clerk said, as she reached for the bell in Emily's hand. As Emily handed it to her, the bell rang quietly again. And as before she felt the same tingle.

"I don't think so." Shocked by her words, Emily stammered, "I don't know why I said that. I love him and I know he loves me. It seems like we're going in that direction."

"I didn't mean to pry, dear, I wish you well. I think you'll know when it's right. You'll have a sign—I'm sure," the woman said in a gentle voice as she wrapped the bell in tissue.

"That's okay and thank you. So how much do I owe you for this?"

"Oh no, it's my gift to you, dear," the elegant clerk said, as she patted the back of Emily's hand. "I think the bell has chosen you."

"What? Oh, please, let me pay for it," Emily said in earnest. As she picked up the bell it began to ring.

"No, but make me a promise that you will listen to the bell

a few times before you gift it. The sound it makes is magic to your heart."

"I will, I promise. Yes, it has the most charming sound. I'm sure Mrs. Hamilton will enjoy it. And I'm so grateful for your generosity." Emily smiled broadly.

"The pleasure is mine. Be very careful on these roads, as you never know what might happen. Take your time and be sure you choose wisely. Merry Christmas, dear."

"And Merry Christmas to you, too, ma'am." Emily wondered what she meant about choosing.

As Emily walked toward the door, she stopped and turned back to face the gracious woman.

"I'm so rude, I didn't introduce myself. My name is—"

"Emily," said the woman, with the sweetest smile and twinkle in her eyes.

"But how do you know—" Emily said, as she stared with a bewildered look on her face. A loud noise startled her from her cloud of confusion. She turned and bumped into a man that just entered the store. Now more rattled than ever, she looked up and gazed into the most striking pale, green eyes she'd ever seen. Not to mention, those eyes were surrounded by a very handsome, smiling face. Emily was speechless, which rarely happened, unless Cooper told her he needed to think, which was much more frequent now.

"I'm so sorry, miss," the stranger said. As his hands touched her arms to steady her, there was a loud ringing from her purse, and she felt a slight flutter. For a moment she was mystified by the sound.

As Emily grasped for words she was struck by the deep resonance of his voice. She thought it sounded like— molasses, thick and sweet. She stood wide-eyed and waited for him to say more. When she gained her senses, she stammered her apologies and lack of etiquette. As she rambled on at this amazingly tall and ruggedly handsome man that stood before her, close enough that she smelled the scent of peppermint on his breath, he raised his hand to quiet her.

"I think that horn is waiting for you, miss," he said, and smiled that crooked smile again.

Emily's face flushed and now she wanted— no, needed— to flee. Cooper honked again before she could get out of the door. The snow and wind had picked up and as it pelted and swirled around her, she shivered. She made her escape and jumped into Cooper's car. In spite of the blast of cold air, her cheeks still felt hot and her heart raced.

Inside Celestial Antiques the young man handed the woman a brightly colored, tin Christmas box. "Merry Christmas, Aunt Estelle. This fudge is from Mom. There's a huge storm on the way. Is there anything I can help you with?"

"No, Andy, I think everything is good with me. Tell your mom I said thanks and Merry Christmas to you both. I'll call if I need your help." She reached in to hug him as she smiled and nodded her head.

"Okay, sounds good. You look beautiful today by the way. And your smile seems to glow even more than usual." Andy smiled, turned and waved as he walked out.

Estelle walked to the store window, put the closed sign up and watched the car drive away. "So, he's the one," she said out loud. "I wonder how the bell will bring them together. I think my work here is done for today." She smiled with a satisfied look. When she locked the front door she looked up at the sign, Celestial Antiques, and pulled her phone from her purse as she walked. "Hello, Elizabeth. I'm just leaving the store and I couldn't wait to tell you. A bell has chosen again— and it's Andy. The red bell." Estelle's voice was excited. "Yes, the one labeled 'love'. I don't know how it will happen but the angels never fail. Okay, stay safe. I love you, too."

❄

"hat took you so long? We have about three more hours of driving through this snow and it's coming down even harder now," Cooper said, as he scowled and pulled away from the curb.

"Sorry, honey, I tried to hurry," Emily said, as she glanced at the clock on the dash. It had only been about fifteen minutes, but seemed much longer, more like a lifetime. She knew that Cooper was annoyed about how the day had gone so far, but he seemed unusually agitated. She'd have to work on managing time better and improve her memory while she was at it. She thought about how she had forgotten Mrs. Hamilton's gift at home. How did that happen? Oh, the coffee, she had filled her mug while she spoke with Sally and set it by her purse. When Cooper honked, she grabbed her purse, suitcase and mug by the door. She wished he wouldn't do that, it always flustered her. He was such a stickler about time and would often start honking when it wasn't necessary or even earlier than needed. She'd have to ask him again not to honk; he had only recently started this habit in the last couple of months. She actually was never late when he wasn't around to blare his horn, and she was sure her neighbors didn't appreciate it. She knew he'd been under a lot of pressure lately at work, but so had she. Then she remembered her encounter at the door, those eyes... that face... and voice. She smiled as she thought perhaps the handsome stranger was a Hollywood actor passing through on vacation. Maybe he was traveling—

"What are you thinking about?" Cooper said, his voice more calm than earlier.

Emily snapped back to where she was and who she was with. Her face flushed and she was glad he hadn't looked at her.

"Oh, um, the lady at that antique store, she was very kind but rather curious. She told me a story about the bell—"

"A bell? You bought a bell for my mother, like one to summon a butler?" Cooper interrupted. "That's a silly gift, I doubt she'll like it. She's not much into antiques unless, perhaps, they come from Christie's. Besides, on your salary you don't need to worry about a gift for her."

"It didn't cost anything, she gave it to me," Emily shot back, annoyed at Cooper's comments.

"Oh, I'd check it out then, it was probably made in China. My mother detests that, it makes her angrier than cold food and she'll be highly offended by it."

"No more than me right now," Emily said, as she pouted. She looked down as her excitement faded and she sighed. Cooper was so intent on the big, future picture that he seemed to find her small joys trivial, as if the little things and small moments that life surprised you with were of no consequence and didn't matter.

"It's the thought that counts, Cooper," Emily said, in her defense.

Cooper snickered. "The only thing my mother counts is money." His phone rang again.

Emily didn't feel like having a conversation about his family and she knew he wasn't in the mood, either. There had seemed to be a formality in his home and with his parents, something not quite comfortable, but she thought it was just her not knowing how ultra-rich people lived their lives. She clearly had no knowledge of that lifestyle, as her parents hadn't been poor, but absolutely not rich, and they hadn't owned a stable of thoroughbred horses. But she'd grown up in a happy, playful household with a family that wasn't afraid to show their affection for one another. Her dad would tease them all, especially her mom. She and her sister would join in and only stop when they made her laugh so hard, she would start to cry. Then Emily's heart sank, as she remembered they were no longer here to hug, talk with and tease. She sighed and looked out the window so Cooper wouldn't see her tears.

The snowbanks were taller, and it appeared the road a bit narrower as they continued up the mountain.

*T*hey drove for a while when Emily felt the car slide a bit. She hadn't noticed that the car moved much faster than before.

"Cooper, please, don't drive so fast on this road. You know it scares me. It's not—"

"Are you saying that I don't know how to drive?" Cooper snapped. "If we hurry, we'll be able to make up some time and just be fashionably late."

"Please—please, slow down, Cooper," Emily begged, her eyes wide with fear.

"Oh, don't be so dramatic," said Cooper, as he glanced at her.

Emily looked at the road and shrieked. Cooper saw the deer, slammed his foot on the brakes and jerked the steering wheel, everything you shouldn't do on snow and ice. The deer jumped into the woods on the other side of the road while the car plowed into the snow-covered ditch with a loud crunch. Emily and Cooper's seat belts locked, and their air bags deployed.

Seconds later, Emily's eyes fluttered as she tried to open them. She could hear Cooper's voice, but she couldn't yet see him. She tried to move her hand, but something stopped it. She heard a whooshing noise and detected the smell of smoke, which frightened her further. She felt groggy, her head pounded, and her body hurt each time she inhaled.

"Emily—Em," she heard Cooper yell. Funny, he never called her Em. He said he didn't like nicknames, his parents never called him Coop, nor did his friends. She had done that once, but only once after his reprimand.

"Emily, are you okay?" Cooper repeated. His airbag had

deflated, and he was able to unlock his seat belt first, so he pushed his door open and crawled out of the car to help Emily. But the car was at a sharp angle in the ditch with the passenger side buried deep in the snow, up to the front wheel well. There was no way to open her door. Emily's airbag had malfunctioned and not deflated as quickly as his. He hurried to get back in the car to check on her.

"Did we hit the deer?" Emily said, in a weak voice. "And why do I smell smoke?"

Cooper checked his phone but there was no service and there was nothing he could do to save them.

"The smell is from the airbags. No, we didn't hit the deer, but I think we hit a big rock under the snow, we're stuck and I'm not sure we could even drive the car if we could get it out. Are you hurt?"

"I'm not sure. There's no blood but my head aches and I feel like someone, or something really big kicked me in the chest."

"Yeah, that's from the airbags. Can you move all your body parts? Does anything feel broken?" Cooper said, concern written on his face.

"I can move but everything above my waist hurts. I'm not sure I should try to get out yet, besides, it's cold out there and I'm already getting chilled." Emily focused her eyes to look out the windshield. "The snow is coming down hard now."

"I know, I'm so sorry. I shouldn't have driven that fast, you were right. I'm such an idiot, I could have seriously hurt or killed you. This day hasn't turned out as expected at all. I should have stuck with the original plan." Copper's face was distraught.

Emily didn't take any satisfaction from his words, her head pounded too much to think about anything else. As Cooper unlatched her seat belt, he put his extra jacket over her.

"This should help you warm up," Cooper said, worried about their situation.

"Speaking of help, did you call 911?" Emily said, with a pained tone.

"We have no cell service, probably because of the mountains and snow." Cooper looked behind them. He thought he had seen headlights coming but then nothing appeared.

"What are we going to do, Cooper?" Emily's voice was more than worried.

"I don't know, there have only been a couple other cars on this road since we've been on it. I guess we'll just have to wait and hope for another car to come by." Cooper's voice was anxious.

Cooper had never been without a plan before, life to him was a gigantic schedule perfectly mapped out. It seemed now this wasn't a plan; it was only luck—if someone came by. He had acted foolishly because of his anger and it could have cost them their lives. It was only supposed to be a four hour drive on the freeway, so they weren't prepared for an emergency like this. They had no food, only half-bottles of water and no blankets. He hadn't planned on driving in a blizzard, through deep snow on a rural road. Bottom line—he hadn't planned. Time stood still. The look on Cooper's face was one that was quite unfamiliar to him as he sat in the car—it was panic.

Twenty cold minutes passed when Emily caught a glimpse of headlights in the rearview mirror.

"Cooper, there's a car coming. Quick, turn the flashers on."

Cooper reacted and shook his head; the situation was dire. His face was pale but not from the cold conditions.

The headlights came and went out of sight as the vehicle drove through the winding curves and then they were clearly headed straight toward them.

Cooper grabbed Emily's scarf and stood behind their car. He waved his arms and the scarf to get the driver's attention.

"Oh, please—please—help us," Cooper said out loud to no one but himself.

The dark blue Bronco slowed and stopped. The tall, dark-haired stranger jumped out of the vehicle and rushed toward Cooper. "Is anyone hurt?" Andy said, his voice urgent.

"I don't think so, not seriously. But my girlfriend hasn't gotten out of the car yet because of the cold. She said that her head hurts and she has a lot of pain in her chest."

Andy pushed past Cooper, to the driver's door. When he opened it, he and Emily were both surprised.

"Well—hello," Andy said, in a low, deep voice as he crawled toward Emily. She was so shocked to see the handsome stranger, with the molasses voice, that she didn't reply. All she could give him was a weak smile.

"Do you feel like anything is broken? How bad does your head hurt? Is there a really sharp pain when you inhale?"

Emily was distracted by that voice again. And. Those. Eyes. After a couple of seconds, she found her voice and composure.

"Let's see. No. Moderately. And all the time," Emily said, with great inner effort and a huge smile.

Andy hesitated for a moment and then smiled back. "Well, at least your sense of humor hasn't been injured."

Emily winced as she laughed and held her ribs.

"I think it only hurts when I breathe hard, so I'd appreciate it if you didn't make me laugh."

"You started it," Andy grinned and stuck out his hand as best he could in the cramped space. "My name's Andy."

Emily took Andy's hand and felt the warmth of his touch and a slight tingle. She didn't hear the ringing in her purse. "Hello, my name is Emily. And you've met Cooper?" Emily asked, as she motioned to the rear seat where he sat.

"Not formally, no. Hey, Coop," Andy said, and looked in

the rearview mirror as he smiled. Cooper returned his gaze but didn't respond or return the smile.

Andy ignored the non-reply and continued with the attractive woman with the delightful sense of humor. "So, follow my finger with only your eyes," Andy said, as he fixed his gaze on her amber eyes and moved his index finger from side to side. "Your vision seems to be tracking okay. Do you feel nauseous or dizzy?"

"No, neither," Emily said. "Are you a doctor?"

"No, but I had some emergency medical training in the military. There weren't always medics around when stuff happened." Andy's face grew more serious. "I was checking for any signs of concussion. The headache is one of the symptoms, but it could also be whiplash." Andy had already assessed that the car would need to be towed. And there was no way to get the passenger door open.

"Coop, grab whatever you need and put it in my rig. Emily, I'm going to lower this seat and move it back. I'm going to turn the key on, and I want you to do the same thing to your seat. Okay?"

Emily nodded and waited for him to turn the key so the seats could be moved.

"Now we need to get you out. Do you think you can move your legs and feet over the console and face me?" Andy said. "I'm right here, I can help you. Once you're in the right position, I'll reach in and lift you out."

Emily heard Andy but hesitated. Her head throbbed and it was difficult for her think clearly.

"Emily? Are you okay to move?" Andy asked, more concerned.

"Oh, yes," she answered and handed him her purse.

"Hand me anything else you want to take; I'll give them to Coop."

"Okay," Emily couldn't help but smile. She knew Cooper was annoyed each time Andy called him by an abbreviation of his name but now was not the time to correct their knight in shining armor. She looked out of the window and saw the vehicle Andy drove. A Bronco. A horse. Knight? Horse? She smiled at the weak joke that she didn't dare to share out loud. She was just glad Cooper hadn't said anything about his nickname.

"*T*hat's everything," she said to Andy, as she handed off the last of her personal belongings.

"Now move slowly and if you have any sharp pain, stop until it subsides. It may be easier to move your legs over first. One at a time. Okay?"

"Got it," Emily said, as she lifted her left leg and turned toward her rescuer. Her ribs hurt when she moved, so she stopped momentarily before she placed her foot on the driver's seat.

"You okay?" Andy asked, as he looked into her gold-colored eyes welled with tears.

"Yes. I was just doing as I was instructed," Emily said, pain etched on her face.

Andy's crooked smile flashed at her and her ribs hurt a little less.

"Good, just take it slow. See if you can get your other leg over now. Good. Hey, Coop, open the back passenger door on my Bronco when I have Emily out of the car."

"Okay, I'm ready," Cooper answered, as his eyes narrowed at the command.

"Emily, now I'm going to reach in, and I want you to wrap your arms around my neck as I lift and pull you out."

"Okay, I'm ready," Emily said, as she mentally braced herself for the pain.

As Andy reached in to pick her up, she wrapped her arms around his neck. With his face close to hers, she smelled peppermint again. But she forgot about that the moment he lifted her and moved her out of the door. She flinched as her ribs screamed at the movement.

"I'm sorry, Emily, I'll have you down in a minute. I promise." Andy's face looked worried, but his deep voice soothed her frazzled nerves and his strong arms gave her comfort.

Emily nodded and laid her cheek on his shoulder as tears streamed down her face. Cooper opened the door as Andy turned and lifted her up. He ever so gently set her down on the back seat and moved her legs into the vehicle. Emily exhaled as the pain backed off. Cooper stood to the side and watched as he held her purse.

"Emily, can I get you something?" Cooper's anxiety had peaked as evidenced by his squeaky voice. "Do you want your purse?" Emily nodded. When she took her purse, she heard the bell again ever so faint. As Andy leaned toward her, she felt her pulse quicken.

"You okay?" Andy said. His brows were furrowed as he spoke, and his voice was low and calm as he looked her in the eyes, compassion on his face.

"Yes. I just need to find a comfortable position again; parts of me hurt more than I realized. Maybe I can lie down, that might help take the pressure off of my ribs."

"Wait, don't move, I'll fix you up." Andy reached over the back seat and pulled a bag from behind her. Inside the duffel was a blanket and down jacket. Andy rolled the jacket into a pillow and placed it on the seat as he reached over her. The scent of peppermint distracted her mind for a moment, and she smiled to herself.

"Okay, scoot over a little and I'll move your legs up while you lie down." Andy carefully lifted her legs onto the seat. "Is that good?"

"Yes, that's better," Emily replied. "I'll need that blanket for sure, though." Emily shivered as she held her arms across her chest. Cooper watched over Andy's shoulder but then jumped into the truck.

"Absolutely, this is why I keep these things in my Bronco, for emergencies just like this." Andy shook the blanket open and laid it over Emily. "Are you comfortable, is that better?" Andy tucked the blanket around Emily's body to trap in the warmth. Emily couldn't remember the last time anyone had tucked her in. This wasn't actually a bed, but his actions made her feel special and cared for.

"Do you hear a bell ringing?" Andy asked as he looked at Emily's purse. "I'm not the one who got hit in the head, so—" he said and laughed.

"It's a bell in my purse that I bought in town," Emily said. "Strange how it seems to just randomly ring by itself." She smiled up at Andy and shrugged.

"Emily, do you need some water?" Cooper said, from the front passenger seat. He handed the bottle back to her. "Just try to relax for now. Let me know if you need anything else, okay?" Cooper smiled weakly and spoke with a squeaky voice.

"Okay." She reached for the water and took a long drink. She hadn't realized she was so thirsty. It had been a long, eventful and dreadful day and it wasn't yet over.

Andy left the truck running so once everyone was in and the doors closed, Emily soon began to warm up. Her head ached but at least her chest wasn't as painful as it had been earlier. She sighed and tried to release the tension in her body. Images from the day flashed through her mind. The lady at the antique store. The wonderful fragrances she smelled there. Why was that star on the tree so radiant? And Andy... she closed her eyes and drifted off before the scene of the accident interrupted her thoughts again and filled her with fear.

"Your Bronco is an old beast, but it looks to be in pretty good condition," Cooper said. His attempt at small talk didn't sit well with Andy, whose face instantly grew annoyed.

"Yeah, she's a bit old but she's not broken and sitting in a snowbank in the middle of nowhere," Andy said with veiled hostility. "My dad and I spent three years restoring this baby, but I have a lifetime of memories from my time with him."

Cooper's expression fell. "I didn't mean to offend you, Andy. I can't even begin to thank you enough for saving us," Cooper said. "I'm not sure what we would have done, especially since Emily is hurt."

"No problem," Andy said, the annoyance of Cooper's remark still on his face. "So, I'm taking you both home with me to my mom's house. She owns Betsy's B&B so there's plenty of room for you. In the winter there are few guests and none right now. You're just lucky that my mom needed a few things from town at the last minute, before the sheriff decided to close the roads. He put the sign up when I left, so I was the last car headed in this direction. And Sheriff Thomas, in Oakville, had already put up signs to block traffic coming from the other way. Sheriff Ben said this storm is going to be a monster, so he wanted to stop all traffic. Just yesterday it didn't look so bad, but you know how nature changes your plans, right? It's supposed to dump about three feet of snow up here, so no sense trying to clear anything until this is over. Everyone in these parts just loads up on supplies and rides it out. We're used to these winter squalls. So, was it a deer that caused the accident?" Andy asked.

By the look on his face Andy's question surprised Cooper. "How did you know?"

"When I looked at the front of your car for damage, I saw deer tracks. That happens a lot in this area, that's why it's a good idea to take it slow on this stretch of the road. One jumped out in front of me, too, not long ago. But I expected it would happen someday, so I drive pretty cautiously through here."

"Yeah, it really surprised me, I guess I didn't pass the test." Cooper shook his head. "We're on our way to my parents' home for the holidays. I'll need to let them know as soon as possible about what happened and where we are now. I tried my cell phone to dial 911 but there's no service."

"Here, you can use my satellite phone." Andy reached into the side pocket of his door and handed it to Cooper. "Several of us in this community have these, including Sheriff Murphy. It's a way to make sure we're all safe and taken care of, especially my mom. She's my cook, I can't let anything happen to her." Andy winked and smiled. "I also installed a booster at home, so you'll be able to use your cell and the internet."

"Oh, and is there any way to get Emily to a doctor?"

"Nope, not with the road closures. But my mom has lived in the country most of her life and knows how to diagnose and treat almost anything. She'd gone to medical school before she married my dad so she's a pretty darn good doctor's assistant. In fact, she's even helped other folks after she's conferred with Dr. Michaels by phone. Some people live in really remote places here and mom's house is about halfway between both towns. The community would have a hard time without her. Besides, she never charges them, and the doc keeps her closet filled with medical supplies, that's the way it works here. If there's a real emergency, she'll prep patients for the ride to the doctor's office."

"That's an interesting arrangement. I don't think I could live so far off the grid, though. I've always had a city way of life and that's where I need to be professionally," Cooper said.

Cooper's looks, mannerisms and the fact that he drove a late model BMW were a dead giveaway that he was a rich, city boy.

"Well, to each his own and whatever makes them happy," Andy said. "Hey, you better call your parents. I'm sure they'll be worried when you don't make it there."

Andy's last words jolted Cooper upright and his face

reflected the seriousness of his current crisis. He called his father to tell him the news of their delayed arrival.

After a thirty-minute drive Andy slowed at a blue sign that read 'Walkers Meadow' and made a right turn onto a smaller, winding road with much deeper snow. There were large stands of leafless trees and snowbanks on both sides.

"How much longer before we get there?" Cooper asked as he watched them go deeper into the wilderness.

"About another fifteen minutes. It's good Emily is resting; that gives her injured muscles a chance to relax. That must have been pretty frightening for her."

"Unfortunately for us I decided to try the side road because there was a big accident on the highway with a long delay expected. I gambled and lost, and that usually doesn't happen. Guess I should have waited there and not been impatient. Now my car's wrecked, we're stranded and at your mercy." The look of resignation on Cooper's face told the story of plans gone awry.

"Well, consider this a surprise part of your vacation. You'll like my mom and her B&B. And like I said earlier, she's the cook and an amazing one at that; you'll probably gain some weight while you're here." Andy chuckled to lighten the conversation. "I'm sure you've stayed in some world-class hotels, but they have nothing on Betsy's B&B, you'll see."

4

*E*mily woke and moaned as she tried to move. She'd slept in the same position for the entire ride and now her muscles had tightened again, only now her neck was stiff, too.

Before Cooper said anything, Andy spoke up. "How are you doing back there? Pretty sore, huh?" He watched her in the rearview mirror and smiled.

"I'm not sure yet. Let me die first, then I'll tell you," Emily moaned again.

"Well, you haven't lost your sense of humor, that's a good sign. I told Coop that my mom's a pretty good witch doctor and she'll take good care of you." Andy snickered.

"I can hardly wait. Hey, when are we going to be wherever it is you're taking us?"

"We'll be at my mom's B&B in just a few minutes. You'll like her, she's the best and the house is fantastic. During the summer she's pretty busy with lots of guests who come here for the scenery, hiking and fishing. It's actually a travel destination."

Emily's chest hurt when she giggled. "You sound like a TV commercial."

Andy laughed. "Well, it's the truth, it's wonderful here. In my humble opinion, it's truly a bit of heaven."

Cooper didn't look very amused by their conversation, especially the topic. "Scenery, hiking and fishing would never make it to my bucket list," Cooper said. "I went marlin fishing once down in Mexico and there wasn't any part of that trip I considered enjoyable. I only agreed to go because I hoped to impress a former girlfriend's father. At the time it seemed like a good business move but it didn't pan out, because in the end, I didn't catch a fish or the girl." Cooper laughed at his story, but he was the only one.

As the truck rounded a curve, it slowed and a large, snow-filled meadow came into view. It was beyond imagination and a breathtaking sight to behold. Near the eastern edge was a flat-topped hill upon which perched a glorious Victorian styled house, behind which stood a barn and several outbuildings. The house was dramatic and striking in contrast to the untouched, white canvas of snow. The dark blue-gray, grand and stately home had two stories. It was replete with a steep, gabled roof, dormer and bay windows, and most stunning of all was the additional two-story tower.

Andy stopped the truck, as he wanted his guests to take in the unexpected beauty of Betsy's B&B. "And I present to you —my mom's house." Andy smirked as he gestured toward the meadow.

By now Emily was in a seated position and was astounded by what she saw, the amazement clearly written on her face.

"Oh, my goodness," she breathed. "There is no word I can think of to do justice to how magnificent this is. It's a postcard or a Michelangelo painting or—it's just unbelievable."

"Very impressive for being in the middle of nowhere," Cooper said wryly. The trite comment bounced off of Andy as he showed he was more interested in Emily's reactions.

"Yeah, it is pretty amazing alright." Andy looked in the

mirror and gazed at the excitement on Emily's face and smiled.

"I can hardly wait to see it up close. I bet the interior is stunning," Emily said with excitement in her voice.

"This was my mom's dream that my dad and she made come true. It was a long, hard project that took many years to complete, but together it was their labor of love."

Cooper seemed bored again with the conversation and looked at his Rolex, the time on his phone and the many messages he'd missed that urgently needed attention. He put his phone to his ear to listen to his voicemail, as he eyed Emily and Andy.

When Andy put the truck in drive and continued toward the house, Emily couldn't look away from the fairy tale scene and he smiled at her girlish enthusiasm. Cooper had his head down and looked deep in thought as he scribbled notes on a small pad, unaffected by the merriment of the other two passengers.

As Emily stared at the large house, she clasped her hands together.

"I've only seen pictures of houses like this in movies or magazines. Oh my, and I've always wondered - what's in the tower, Andy?" She looked at Andy in the mirror and grinned.

"My dad loved books of all kinds and my mom loved anything related to travel and medicine, so the bottom floor is a huge library. And I have a desk in there and space that serves as my office, too. The top floor is the master suite for my mom. But just wait until you see the view from the library, it is truly incredible, and you'll see the world with fresh eyes and a new perspective."

Emily giggled and grinned. "I might need some oxygen then because this already has me breathless, I'm not sure I can take any more."

"Maybe we should blindfold you so we don't overload

your senses. We wouldn't want you to faint," Andy laughed as he watched Emily grin at him in the mirror.

*E*mily's eyes were transfixed on the house until a stand of trees blocked the view. As Andy passed the trees, he stopped again at more of a side view of the house and the expanse of snow below. The meadow had several groups of smaller trees and bushes which the wildlife used for food, shelter and to stalk their prey.

"If you look closely at the base of that first group of shrubs, you'll see lots of different tracks in the snow leading in and out. That's the hiding place for lots of smaller animals like snowshoe hare, squirrels and fox. Other creatures you might see in the meadow, if you're lucky enough, are deer, elk, and an occasional bobcat. I've enjoyed watching how all the animals interact and what their habits are. This meadow is a microcosm for how life depends on the existence of other living things, it's a miniature world of its own and a reflection of the big picture." Andy's voice was filled with fondness as he looked back at a smiling Emily.

"I already know I'll be spending a lot of time looking out of those windows. But right now, I'm captivated by and appreciating the exterior of that lovely house."

Emily marveled at the architectural design with the wrap-around porch, second-story balcony, and the dome-shaped gazebo. The white ornamental spindles that surrounded the porch, in addition to the white carved brackets, ornate trim and scalloped shingles added exquisite detailing. The distinctive windows varied in shapes and sizes with arches, decorative panels, eyebrows and stained glass. She grinned and clapped at the weathervane on top of the pointed roof of the tower, it was a copper angel blowing a trumpet. The ornately structured house honored and hearkened back to a time in history when architectural craftsmanship was an art and each home distinctly unique.

"I don't think you've blinked once since we stopped," Andy laughed as he watched her expressions and listened to her sounds of delight.

Emily giggled and said, "I'm afraid I'll miss something, the more I look the more I see, it's like a fantasy and it's cast a spell on me. I'll cherish this moment forever. But I'm afraid it'll disappear before I can go inside."

Andy grinned a crooked smile into the mirror and continued toward the house, immersed in Emily's joy.

5

*A*s the Bronco approached the house, an excited dog ran out to greet them. Emily loved dogs but living in the city, and her long hours at work, made it impossible for her to have one. For her eighth birthday her parents let her adopt a dog from the shelter. The dog looked like a little dust mop and wouldn't stop licking Emily's face on the ride home, happy to no longer be confined to a cage. Emily named her Muffin because as soon as she entered the house, she stole her dad's muffin he'd left sitting on the coffee table. Her dad was especially unhappy because it was the last one. Muffin was her constant companion and best friend until Emily had gone away to college. She missed that unconditional love dogs have for their human friends. When Emily was sad or had a bad day Muffin would be by her side, she always knew Emily's moods and acted accordingly. Emily was certain that Muffin could have received a high school diploma, too, had she been able to talk. Muffin helped her study for every algebra and Spanish test. When Emily practiced her oral presentations, Muffin sat and listened and blinked her approval. The day her mom called, when Muffin died, Emily felt she had lost a part of her heart and her childhood. But, since that time of sadness, she had instituted a new tradition. She thought of her little friend every day that she stopped at the coffee shop and bought a muffin with her latte and she'd smile at the memories. "Here's to you Muffin," Emily would say as she held the small, delicious cake up in the air before she took her first bite. She often got sideways glances from those around her but that didn't matter. The tradition to honor her furry friend was meant to live on and it brought her joy.

The black and white dog crisscrossed in front of the truck a couple of times, careful to keep its distance, then ran to the porch, sat down and barked twice as its tail wagged furiously.

"That's Lady," Andy said, "she's the resident alarm, guard dog, greeter and hostess. She was my dad's companion, now her job is to welcome guests and announce their arrivals." Seconds later a tall, attractive woman, with long, auburn hair, appeared on the porch and stood next to Lady. "And that is my mom," Andy said, with a tender voice tinged with pride. Andy's love for his mother was more than evident and Emily's eyes filled with tears.

Emily leaned forward and moaned as she did. "Wait," Emily said, alarmed. "She looks just like the woman in the antique store. I know I've been hit in the head but I'm not imagining this, am I?" Emily's eyebrows furrowed as she stretched to look closer.

Andy laughed and said, "I wondered if you'd notice. Yes, they're sisters, twins in fact. People in town get them mixed up all the time so my Aunt Estelle wears her hair up and my mom keeps hers down when she's in public. They really do look alike, don't they?"

"It's truly incredible and with that same warm, welcoming smile."

Andy parked near the house where an area had been cleared and a path in the snow led to the house. He jumped out of the truck, as he yelled, "Hey, Mom, I brought some house guests home for you."

Without hesitation his mom waved and grinned. "That's perfect, Andy, I have a big pot of stew cooking as we speak. Also, some fresh baked bread like I promised you for going to town at the last minute."

"Not a problem, Mom, anything for you—even without bread, but the food sounds great. I'm starving and I'm sure these folks are hungry and ready to get out of this truck." Andy and his mom laughed. She came down the stairs with Lady beside her, the dog careful not to get in front of her and cause her to fall.

Cooper had gathered his belongings in the front and gotten out of the Bronco as Betsy approached. He squared his shoulders and lifted his chin a bit.

"Mom, this is Cooper. Cooper, this is Betsy, the owner of this highly esteemed bed and breakfast," Andy said, as he smiled.

Cooper held out his hand, but Betsy reached up with her arms and gave him a hug instead.

"Glad to meet you and happy to have you here," Betsy said warmly. Cooper looked surprised and acted like he wasn't sure what to do at first. But he then returned her hug, just not with as much enthusiasm. Lady, however, had approached Cooper, dropped her wagging tail and backed away. Betsy didn't hear the low rumble in Lady's chest, who normally was friendly to new people, but she was cautious about this new man.

As Andy opened the rear door, he made more introductions.

"And, Mom, this is Emily. Emily, this is Betsy, CEO of this country enterprise." Andy laughed at his own joke and grinned. "I found these fine people stuck in a snowbank on my way back home. Their car was too damaged to drive, and Ben had already closed the road back to Parsons, anyway. They'll be here until the storm passes and other arrangements for transportation can be made. Also, Emily has some injuries you'll need to look at, Mom. I think maybe whiplash or mild concussion and bruised ribs from the airbags."

"Oh my, don't worry dear, we'll get you all fixed up," Betsy said to Emily. "Can I help carry anything? Here, let me take your purse while Andy helps you get out of there." Betsy grabbed the purse and heard a tinkling sound—she smiled.

Andy helped Emily turn her legs and reached in to pick her up. Cooper had just carried their bags to the porch and slipped off the bottom stair but managed not to fall.

"I can help Emily," Cooper said, as he hurried to reach the truck.

"I think I better do it. Your shoes aren't the best on this snow and ice, I'd hate for both of you to be injured," Andy said. "But you can close the door after I get Emily out. And, please, grab anything else that should come in the house, too."

"I think I can walk, Andy," Emily said.

They both looked down at her shoes. Her leather heels were pretty and good for city sidewalks and offices but not exactly the best choice to trek through snow.

"Not gonna happen," Andy said. "Just wrap your arms around my neck like before and I'll carry you into the house. Okay?"

Emily nodded, reached up her arms and winced when Andy lifted her up. "I'm sorry, Em, but don't worry, I've got you." As Andy carried her into the house, she felt that same sense of security as she had earlier that day. She sighed and wished the house was further away.

Betsy stood ready to open the door for her son and the injured guest. Andy took a few steps inside then carefully set Emily down on her feet. For a moment their eyes met as they exchanged barely perceptible smiles.

"Where should I put these suitcases," Cooper said, and interrupted the moment.

"You can set them at the base of the stairs over there," Betsy said. She'd also observed the look between the two and Emily's flushed cheeks. "And there's a bathroom close by if you'd like to wash up for dinner. We'll do that right after I take a look at Emily."

"Okay, that sounds good," Cooper said, as he carried the bags across the room.

"Thank you, Andy, for today," Emily said. Andy stood in front of her and was still holding her arms to help her balance.

"Of course, always," Andy said. "Are you okay to stand by yourself? Do you want to sit down? Should I carry you to the chair?"

"Let's see. Yes. No. And no." Emily giggled and then grabbed her chest. "Ow, don't ask so many questions at one time, it makes me laugh."

"That's my girl," Andy said. He smiled and let go of her arms.

"Okay, my turn," Betsy said with a grin and moved between them. "I need to assess Emily's injuries before anything else and that includes fresh baked bread, young man. Follow me to the kitchen, dear."

*E*mily hadn't yet looked in great detail at her new surroundings, but she noticed how large the living room was and a beautifully decorated Christmas tree in the corner by the fireplace. But she felt a warmth, more than just from the burning logs, perhaps it was the genuine hospitality. The women walked across the room at a slow pace, as Emily followed Betsy. The high arched doorway led into an expansive kitchen and dining area. At the far end were tall, arched

French doors that led to the gazebo. It looked like a magazine layout for Better Homes and Gardens—the Victorian edition.

"Have a seat over here, dear. Let me get my exam sheet from Dr. Michaels and ask you some questions. I'll confer with him later about my diagnosis and treatment. The doc is a terrific guy and we work well together to make sure everyone in the community receives medical attention, especially during bad weather." After a brief exam and questionnaire, Betsy had her diagnosis.

"Well, that airbag kept you from more serious injury but did some damage when it deployed, but I don't need to tell you that because you were on the receiving end. We can't take any x-rays, but I'm pretty sure nothing is broken. It looks and sounds like what you have are bruised and strained muscles and soft tissue damage in your chest, shoulders and neck, with some whiplash and slight concussion. Also, most probably, some inflammation has already started in those muscles. Best treatments will be over the counter pain medicine, ice packs for today, and lots of rest. Depending on the extent of the injuries, it could take a couple to several weeks for you to feel back to normal. Also, a long, hot bath before bed might be beneficial. But definitely no lifting and very little movement for now. I'll call the doctor after dinner."

"Wow, this isn't how I thought this vacation would start," Emily lamented.

"Well, now you have the perfect excuse to do absolutely nothing, dear. Here's some water and something to ease the pain. Just a warning, mornings will be the most difficult for a while, your body will scream at you for moving. I'd recommend a hot bath first thing in the morning, too, to loosen the muscles and calm down the pain."

Emily's smile reflected her appreciation. "That's a plus. Doing nothing sounds great, but the pain—not so much. I can't thank you enough, Betsy, or Andy for your help."

"It's our mission in life to help when we see a need, it's in our DNA," Betsy chuckled. "There's a small bedroom downstairs that would be good for you in your condition, because the stairs might be too painful for now, and it's close to the kitchen and fireplace, my two favorite rooms in this big old house," Betsy said. "However, it has a small bed that we sometimes use for guests who don't want to walk up the stairs or for quick naps. Cooper can stay in one of the large suites upstairs. That's the best plan, I hope that's okay?"

"Sounds great. Right now, I'll do anything to keep my ribs from hurting. Cooper might not be so happy but he's not the one who got banged up, besides his decisions led to all this chaos. On the other hand, meeting you and Andy may be the saving grace in all this," Emily said and smiled. Betsy gave her a quick hug.

The men sat quietly in the living room and drank the coffee Andy made for them, as they watched the fire crackle and waited for more instruction from Betsy.

Betsy led Emily to her temporary quarters and asked Cooper to take her suitcase to the room. "After you take Emily's things to her, I'll show you to your room upstairs," Betsy called after him.

Cooper hesitated but was out of hearing distance and continued to Emily's room.

"Right now, Cooper, it hurts for me to even breathe so going up and down the stairs is not an option for me. This is only temporary and the most logical solution for both of us, you'll have everything you need in your room. Hopefully I'll feel better in a few days," Emily explained and watched as the irritation grew on his face.

"I'll work on a plan tomorrow and find out how soon we can get out of here," Cooper said, as he gave Emily a quick kiss and left without asking her more about her injuries.

6

"*P*lease, set the table for me, Andy," Betsy said. "Oh wait, take this tea first to Emily and these ice packs. Tell her to put them on the most painful parts of her body. Then let our guests know that dinner will be ready in twenty minutes."

Andy knocked on Emily's door. For some reason he now felt a bit shy, and he was never shy. But there was something about Emily that had already left an indelible impression, her wit, sweet nature, and ability to make him smile.

"Come in," Emily said. She was reclined on the bed with a comforter over her and a couple of pillows behind her back.

"Betsy wanted you to have some tea, it's chamomile to help you relax. Also, she said to apply these ice packs for a while. Are you comfortable? Well, as much as possible," Andy said, he felt that was a silly question under the circumstances.

"Yes, thank you. That was very sweet of your mom, you're right, she's the best. And I'll be very comfortable here, it feels better than home." Emily smiled.

"Mom said that dinner will be ready in twenty minutes. If you fall asleep don't worry, the kitchen is open for you at any time. There are always leftovers, in fact stew is better reheated. I can't promise I won't eat all the fresh bread, though, it's my favorite." Andy grinned. "I'll see you in a bit, then."

"Don't worry about me being late to the table. I'm famished, I haven't eaten all day."

"You should have said something. Our home is your home and, please, feel free to forage," Andy said with a grin. "I'll let you rest now and enjoy that tea. But seriously, please, let me know if there's anything you need." Their eyes locked for several seconds.

"I will. And, Andy—thank you for everything," Emily said with a warm smile.

Andy gave her a slight bow and backed out of the doorway with a grin.

Andy went upstairs to Cooper's room and knocked. He could hear that Cooper was speaking on the phone. Cooper opened the door with the phone in his hand.

"Hold on, Father," Cooper said as he opened his door. "Yes?" he asked of Andy.

"Sorry to interrupt but dinner will be ready in twenty minutes. Take your time. If you—"

"Okay, thanks," he said to Andy. Without further comment he closed the door on Andy and resumed his phone conversation. "Are you still there? I need to discuss another issue."

Andy stood in the hallway and tried hard not to feel slighted or insulted. He wondered if Cooper treated everyone this way. And he, also, wondered what Emily saw in the guy besides being flashy, handsome and rich. He sighed as he turned and headed back down the stairs as he shook his head.

As Andy walked into the kitchen to set the table, Betsy looked over her shoulder and saw the agitated look on Andy's face.

"So, what's on your mind, young man?" she said, as she continued with her cooking.

"The more I'm around Cooper the less I like him, and Mr. Money Bags started on the minus scale to begin with," Andy said, his jaws tightened.

"Well, be patient with him, he's found himself in a predicament. It's fortunate for him, and Emily, that you came along. We'll share our home for a few days, and they'll be gone. That's why this house exists, to be a shelter for those lost in a storm."

"Was that another lesson, Mom?" Andy said. They laughed as he walked over and hugged her.

"Of course, it was. You know me, I just can't help it. You will always be my little boy that needs instruction," Betsy said, as she looked up to see Andy's face. "Even if you are six plus feet tall. Now set the table, please." Andy grinned at his mom and thanked God for her. She had always been there for him with her love, wisdom and patience.

Cooper glanced at the phone while he talked with his dad. "We'll have to finish this conversation later. I still don't think I'm ready for such a commitment. It's time for dinner now and I haven't eaten all day because of everything that's happened. I'll call you later. Bye."

Cooper ended the call and checked his appearance in the mirror. In spite of the day's catastrophes he still looked put together. He headed down the stairs to Emily's room, but he heard laughter in the kitchen. When he entered, she was seated at the counter with Andy as they talked with Betsy and the dog seated next to her chair. Cooper had never cared for dogs or any animals. He felt they served no purpose, unless like his dad's horses, they made money.

"Good evening all," Cooper said, as he smiled and looked at Emily seated next to Andy. "Something smells good in here, Betsy. I've heard a rumor about your cooking and I'm more than ready to try some." He walked over to Emily and put his hands on her shoulders. "How are you feeling?" he said, as he kissed her cheek.

"Well, after resting and taking some pain medicine, a bit better. It was pretty awful, though, to get up from the bed," Emily said, and furrowed her brows.

"We heard her moan," Betsy said. "Andy ran in to check on her and he was able to assist. Besides, that kept him away from the bread, but I'm still pretty sure some pieces are missing."

Cooper faced Andy and scowled but said nothing. Emily felt Cooper's grip tighten and she quickly interjected.

"Basically, if I just lie still and don't move or laugh, and do as Betsy says, the pain is more tolerable but that's not much fun. I came out here to be social and to get close to the food and that famous bread." Everyone except Cooper laughed.

"Okay, let's sit down," Betsy said, as she lowered the steaming bowl on to the table. The smell was heavenly. Emily was careful to sit between the two men; she detected a slight hostility from Cooper, and she didn't want it to escalate. She just wanted to enjoy a stress-free dinner, in good company, and not think beyond tonight.

"I can hardly wait to eat. Thank you so much, Betsy," Emily said. "And should I put a couple extra pieces of bread on my napkin before Andy gets to it?" Emily giggled and winced. "I keep forgetting not to laugh."

"Well, laughter is the best medicine," Betsy said, "but, perhaps in this case, maybe not." She winked at Emily and grinned. Emily was careful to only smile.

Before they started to pass the food, Betsy asked that they all bow their heads for grace. She and Andy reached out their hands to Emily and Cooper. Emily welcomed the opportunity with an open heart and smiled as she bowed her head. It was second nature for her, and she felt transported to her parents' table, where she had always felt God's love and protection as a child. Cooper, on the other hand, looked surprised and mildly distressed, but after a few moments' hesitation he reached out his hands. He sighed and looked thankful that he sat between the two women.

"Thank you, Heavenly Father, for this bountiful gift of food," Betsy prayed. "I ask that it nourish our bodies and help us to stay strong. And, thank you, for bringing these guests to our table to share in our blessings. We thank you, in Jesus name. Amen." Two other voices added their amen.

"Okay, let's eat," Betsy said. "Hand me your bowls and I'll put some stew in them for you. And there's more bread where that came from," she said and smiled at Emily. "I know how my boy eats, one loaf for him and one for the table."

Emily looked at Andy and grinned as she took a bite of bread. "Oh, my gosh," she said. "Can I take a loaf to my room? No wonder he's been bragging about this, and the stew is divine."

Cooper, who had been quiet, spoke up. "This just may be the best stew I've ever tasted, and I agree with Emily about the bread. How many loaves did you bake, anyway?"

Cooper relaxed and joined in the conversation, however, he avoided eye contact with Andy.

"I can't tell you enough how much we appreciate your generosity, Betsy. And it's been a long time since I've been able to just sit and enjoy dinner at the table. I'm usually rushed to get back to business, phone calls and meetings." Cooper shook his head slightly and glanced at Emily who listened to his words without a smile.

"How is it that you came to have this house out here?" Cooper said to Betsy.

"My late husband, Hank, made this happen. He knew having a bed and breakfast was my dream. When my parents died, I received a small inheritance that I put into a savings account for the future. Unbeknownst to me, Hank had been putting some money aside. He had been a contractor in Parsons, with a good reputation, so he had lots of work for many years.

One day he said he wanted to show me some property. He brought me out here and said, 'Betsy—this is your future. I'm sure your folks would have been happy to buy this for you. I can see a beautiful Victorian house right over there.' I knew instantly what he meant and was overwhelmed with joy and, of course, tears. We bought the hundred acres and spent the next five years building this house, it became our labor of love." Betsy's voice dropped off as she wiped away a tear. She looked up and smiled. "And I wouldn't give it up for the world because I know this is where I was meant to be. And I believe this is a shelter for weary souls and those stuck in snowbanks." Betsy laughed and winked.

"That's an amazing story, Betsy, thanks for sharing it," Emily said, as she dabbed her eyes. "I can tell that Hank really loved you."

"Yes, he did," Betsy said, as she glanced at Emily and then looked at each person. "And he would have enjoyed this company around the table tonight, too. So—who wants pie? We can take it in the family room by the fireplace."

*C*ooper chose to go up to his room and didn't join the group. He explained he had phone calls that needed to be returned. He gave Emily a quick peck on the cheek and said he'd be down again before she went to bed. She wasn't surprised he'd gone upstairs and she explained to Betsy and

Andy it was his usual routine. The three enjoyed each other's company and the warmth of the burning logs. Probably more so than if Cooper had joined them. He didn't quite seem to fit in, so that caused them all to look a bit uncomfortable.

"That was an extraordinary dinner, Betsy," Emily said, as she finished the last bite of her apple pie. "I'd love to have your recipes—for everything. I'm not a very good cook because I haven't had the time. But actually, I do know fifty ways to cook ramen," Emily laughed at herself and winced. "I need to stop laughing, but it feels good for my soul. Today was so stressful, but you've really helped me feel better. I can't tell you how relaxed and safe I feel here and how very grateful I am."

"We're glad you're here," Betsy and Andy said in stereo. Surprised by it, their eyes widened, then all three laughed.

"Oh, I better go to bed, I can't stand the pain much longer," Emily said, as she grinned and grimaced almost at the same time. "But I'm truly enjoying your company. It's so easy here, I feel like—I belong."

Andy was the first to smile. "You will always be welcome here, dear," Betsy said. "Andy, would you, please, take our plates to the kitchen?"

As Betsy and Emily talked, Emily could hear the sounds of the dishes and kitchen being cleaned. She was impressed, but not surprised as this was a well-functioning family.

The women watched the fire die down and after twenty minutes Emily grew weary and achy. "I think it's time for me to get ready for bed. Maybe I'll take a long bath first, that might ease some of the tightness before I go to sleep."

"There are fresh towels on the small shelf beside the tub, along with some Epsom salt and lavender bath wash. If you need anything else, just holler," Betsy said. "Would you like another cup of chamomile tea?"

"Yes, please, that would be the trifecta of relaxation. You're spoiling me."

"That's what I do best," Betsy said, with a smile. "I'll bring that to you in just a couple of minutes."

"Also, would you please tell Cooper that I've gone to bed. I thought he would have come back down by now," Emily said with disappointment on her face.

"Certainly, dear," Betsy replied in a soft voice.

7

*C*ooper had gone back up to his room and thought about the day while he showered. He shook his head at how quickly the day had deteriorated. He was too tired to make any more phone calls, especially to his father, those conversations were always so draining. And why did Andy get on his nerves? Maybe he was just a little too nice, too eager to please, especially Emily. In any case, he and Emily would leave as soon as the storm passed. Tomorrow he'd make more calls and more money from the deals he had yet to close. But he still couldn't shake the image of how Emily looked at Andy. Obviously, she's just a sucker for a pretty-faced, scruffy, country boy that came to her rescue. But soon enough she'd realize he had nothing to offer her except a big smile and poverty. Cooper struggled with his thoughts as he checked his phone and finally went to bed. As he got in bed, he realized he hadn't gone back downstairs, he should have checked on Emily and made sure she was okay. But Betsy and Andy seemed to have everything under control and would take good care of her, for now.

Cooper thought about the first time he'd seen Emily. He was with his father at the law firm he employed for his brokerage company and financial affairs. It was expected he would someday take over his father's businesses, so he was being introduced to and trained by those who dealt with all the financial transactions. Mr. Hamilton wanted Cooper to gain the respect of those he would someday need to protect his wealth.

Cooper knew by the way the women at the legal offices treated him that he was the big catch. He was handsome, soon to be very rich—and single. The furtive glances that lingered and large smiles were intended to attract him, but he barely acknowledged their existence. He knew the power of his intense blue eyes and wealth.

After an hour into the third day, Cooper's attention began to wander. He yawned and looked across the open office space and noticed a young woman, among several, as she studiously thumbed through a stack of file folders. On occasion she'd stop and take notes, then carry the pile of folders to the elevator. She would return with another stack of folders and repeat the process. He was intrigued, not with what she was doing, but with how stunning she was. Her skin was a light, golden tan and her features were refined and delicate, her full lips in a constant pout as she worked.

At the first opportunity, he asked one of the lawyer's assistants about her.

"Do you know who that woman is at the end of the table across the hallway?"

The assistant saw several. "The blonde? Which one?" she said, with a puzzled look.

"No, the one with the long, dark hair." Cooper realized they were all different shades of blonde except the one he inquired about. Her hair was dark brown with copper highlights that reflected in the sunshine from the windows. She had her hair pulled loosely back and held with a rhinestone clip, the kind from a dollar store. Although her clothes were obviously of lesser quality, her figure was perfectly proportioned and would do justice to any originals from Gucci or Saint Laurent.

The assistant shrugged and said she was just one of the newer paralegals and she had not yet met her. Cooper decided he would create the situation to do that.

He drifted off thinking about Emily—and the engagement ring in his briefcase.

*A*ndy and Betsy finished the dinner cleanup and sat by the fire with their tea. Full and relaxed, they shared some quiet time and exchanged some thoughts of the day's events.

"So, they were just waiting for someone to come by?" Betsy said, as she shook her head.

"There was nothing else they could do, and you know there isn't any cell service there. I guess Emily's angel was watching over them," Andy replied.

"You're very specific about who has an angel, son." Betsy giggled. "Emily is a beautiful young woman, but more importantly she has a good heart and a sweet spirit. But she's also spoken for, Andy."

"I know, Mom, I'm just enjoying her company for the next few days. I'm not ready for any romantic relationship anyway." Andy's voice saddened as he looked at the fire.

"It's been over three years since you and Lisa parted ways. Don't you think it's time to get back out there? You can't hide on this mountain forever, Andy. There's someone out there for you, but you have to be willing to trust again."

"Yeah, that's the hardest part—trust. When I got that Dear John letter while on tour, it's all I could do to stay focused. Taking care of my men, who really needed me, is what helped me deal with the pain and anger. It no longer hurts and I'm no longer angry, but I just can't take that chance again —not yet."

"You're right, I guess you're the only one who can make that decision. I just don't want you to have your heart shut so tightly that no light at all can get in. Do you know what I mean?"

Andy smiled. "I do, Mom, and I love you for it. I promise if I find a woman who can challenge me, I'll take that as a sign that she's the one." He grinned and gave his mom a big hug as he laughed.

"Okay, now you're just making fun of me. Go to bed," Betsy said, as she laughed, too.

"Good night, Mom and thanks for a terrific dinner—especially the bread."

*A*ndy lay in bed and thought about the guys he'd gotten so close to and fought beside in Afghanistan. What he'd seen still haunted him, especially thoughts about Willie. He was the reason that Andy came back home alive and the reason that Willie didn't. Andy would never understand why his friend insisted they exchange seats. The guilt was not as heavy as it had been when he first got back, but he still dealt with it from time to time. He knew he needed to call Angela, Willie's wife, but that was still a little difficult. The day he first saw her, Andy lost it. He had promised her he wouldn't let anything happen to Willie. As soon as he got stateside, he went to see her and when she hugged him and told him it wasn't his fault, the guilt crushed him. He felt she deserved to have her husband and their baby deserved to have her father. They had chosen him as Christina's godfather, and he was there when she was christened. But Andy had failed. Angela knew Andy took her husband's death all on his own shoulders, so she called him almost weekly for the first few months. They shared memories and their grief and as time passed their hearts began to heal. When one of them was overwhelmed by Willie's absence they would call the other for support and this time his call would be for Angela's well-being. Andy thought about the day—and Emily. He felt drawn to her, to more than just her beauty. Her presence seemed to soothe him, and her smile and sense of humor lightened his spirit. He had never felt this way about any other woman before. But she'd leave in a few days and that would be that. But he remembered how he felt when he looked into her eyes, the peace and calm that flooded his senses. He sighed and his mind stilled.

*E*mily had nearly fallen asleep in the bath, but she was relaxed and ready to crawl into bed. When she opened the door she almost stepped on Lady, who waited for her. "I like you too, Lady." She gave the dog some rubs and went to her room. She'd forgotten her lotion in the bathroom and when she opened her bedroom door, Lady was there. "What are you doing Lady, guarding me?" Again, she stroked the dog for a few minutes before she retrieved her lotion. "Thanks, Lady, I'll feel safe with you watching out for me," Emily smiled. It was nice to have some furry companionship again if only for a brief time. With great care Emily got in bed and when she pulled up the comforter, she realized that Lady had been by her side all evening, almost as much as Andy. She smiled with the thought. He was so attentive to her and even laughed at her attempts to be funny. Cooper rarely found her amusing anymore. She wondered what happened to Cooper. Why hadn't he come back to check on her? "Oh well, I think you're better protection than him anyway, Lady," Emily whispered to herself just before she started to dream —about Andy.

$\mathcal{A}$s Betsy got ready for bed she thought about her new guests. Emily was a wonderful person to be around. She had a heart full of love and kindness, but still carried a lot of pain from her parents' passing. And she was young and still finding her way. She hoped Emily would lean on the teachings her family taught her as she'd grown up. She sensed that Cooper, on the other hand, had been taught to serve himself first. And that money and power were the objective and the priority. She suspected he only allowed those people into his world that would somehow help him achieve those goals. She felt Emily was the one good thing in Cooper's life and she hoped Emily could soften his heart with her love. Andy needed that kind of love to help heal the darkness in his heart. He had always been able to share his deepest thoughts with his dad and found just the right advice from him. But Andy's heart had been fractured too many times in the last few years. He didn't show it—but Betsy knew her son. Memories of Hank floated into her mind and she smiled. Her hand moved to touch what had been his side of the bed. She missed him dearly but no longer cried herself to sleep. Her tears had changed to happy memories. She knew she had been the luckiest woman in the world to have slept beside Hank. She thanked God she had been blessed to be his partner for thirty-five years. She fell asleep as she prayed.

8

*A*rthur and Cynthia Hamilton had just bid farewell to their last dinner guests. As they watched from the foyer window, the headlights disappeared as the last car rounded the curve on the long driveway.

"The dinner went well, I think, in spite of Cooper and Emily's absence. Don't you think?" Arthur said to his wife. "I'll call Cooper in the morning and get an update so I can make arrangements to retrieve them. I don't know why your son decided to change his driving plans." Arthur shook his head and pursed his thin lips. He straightened his dinner jacket and squared his shoulders. His temples had grayed but he was still quite the distinguished-looking man of his youth.

"What I think, is that I'll have to plan another get together with the Taylors while Charlotte is in town. It can be another family invitation," Cynthia replied, as she stopped to view herself in the hallway mirror. She tucked a loose blonde hair back into place and adjusted her sequined gown on her still trim figure. "I don't know why this went all wrong tonight; it was planned perfectly, of course."

"You just can't accept that Cooper and Charlotte are no longer together can you? Just let it go, Cooper has moved on.

And a second dinner invitation isn't at all obvious, Cynthia?" Arthur asked. He was perturbed by now at his wife's meddling.

As they walked down the marbled foyer, Arthur saw the butler clearing the dining table. "Ferguson, please bring two brandies to the study for the missus and me. Thank you."

Mr. and Mrs. Hamilton seated themselves near the fireplace in overstuffed, velvet chairs. They both had gotten a bit chilled when they escorted their guests to the door.

"I think Charlotte has matured in the last two years, don't you? It appeared so at dinner tonight, and she looks even more radiant than ever. She seemed very interested in what Cooper was doing these days—and how he was doing. I know she wanted to ask if he was seeing anyone. There's still some interest there, I can tell, Arthur. Her mother told me Charlotte is available and that she knows she made a big mistake not marrying Cooper."

"Well, twenty-twenty hindsight on her part I suppose," Arthur sighed in resignation. Ferguson entered the room with their drinks and set them on the table. "Thank you, Ferguson. That's all for tonight."

"Yes, sir," the butler replied. "Have a good evening," he said, as he bowed to both.

"Look, Cooper has chosen Emily and seems to be happy with her, he's told me that he loves her. She's intelligent, beautiful and has worked hard to further her education and career, I admire that in her. Most of the other women he brought home were only interested in his money and our fortune. I need him to stay on track with my plan. Besides another lawyer in the family might be good. I'm sure Emily will do nothing to embarrass the Hamilton name. Give her a chance, Cynthia." Arthur's expression showed his annoyance at his wife's persistence.

"Well, it's been two years and she still makes mistakes at the dinner table. How confusing can silverware be? I can't help it if I still hope that Cooper and Charlotte get married. They would make such beautiful babies and our two families would carry on the traditions of our lineages," Cynthia said, as she pleaded her case.

"It's history, let it go. Charlotte broke Cooper's heart when she called it off before the wedding. Maybe that's why your son was attracted to Emily so quickly. He didn't think she'd run off with some other rich guy. She's just a poor, working girl who wouldn't let go of a good thing." Arthur was annoyed and wanted to end the conversation. "Look, I need Cooper to stay on track with my plan. There isn't time for him to find another woman, okay? I need him to tie the knot before I present him to the board as my new vice president. If he has a settled appearance, they will be less likely to give me any grief. The board wouldn't approve of a rich playboy at the table or at the helm. Besides, he'll be more focused on business which is what I need him to be."

"I suppose so," Cynthia said, with a flip of her hand in dismissal. "If he's not happy down the road, he can always divorce her in a few years, hopefully before babies because that would complicate matters. That reminds me, Cooper needs a prenup. We don't want Emily to think she's struck oil," Cynthia said snidely.

"I've already drawn it up, I just have to fill in the fiancé's name," Arthur sighed as he rolled his eyes for the millionth time that evening.

Cynthia Hamilton hadn't worked a day in her life, unless you considered husband hunting a job. As far back as she could remember she had been given one mission in life by her parents. She was to go to college, the best school of course, and find a suitable man for marriage. It had been difficult to please her mother and father. She brought home several boys from school, but none met with approval—until Arthur. She attempted many times to catch his eye, she'd even taken classes she had no interest in. He was the biggest prize on campus, so it took her a while. But in the end, she won—big. Her life consisted of entertaining important people and taking opulent vacations, with other rich and affluent women. It suited her just fine that Arthur didn't accompany her, she always had more fun without him. She had made her parents very proud.

Arthur and Cynthia Hamilton led a happy and entitled life. They enjoyed their arrangement, they wanted for absolutely nothing and had everything in excess. Arthur spent most of his day commanding an army of moneymakers. And in any spare time, he attended to his hobby of Kentucky thoroughbreds. Perhaps, his only vice was horse racing but that, too, brought in more money and gave him an opportunity to do business. Yes, Arthur's life had turned out just as his father had planned for him. And now it was his turn to lead his son in the right direction. There was after all a fortune to be maintained.

9

The next morning Betsy was busy in the kitchen and she almost had breakfast prepared when Emily walked in rather carefully and slowly. Lady ran over to greet her, she herself had just come inside the house. Lady spun in circles and whimpered until Emily spoke to her and scratched an ear. "I love you too, Lady." Emily smiled at the attention.

"Whatever you're doing in here smells wonderful," Emily said. She walked, slightly bent over, to the stove and admired the sizzling ham and eggs. "I can't believe I'm hungry after how much I ate last night but my stomach just growled." Emily grinned at the cook. "No matter how much it hurt to get here, the food called to me."

Betsy turned and gave Emily a careful hug. "How are you feeling this morning, Em?" she said. "Pretty banged up I would guess. There's coffee on the island or hot water for tea if you prefer."

"I'm definitely a coffee person first thing in the morning," Emily said, as she grabbed a mug and filled it. As she poured, she realized Betsy had called her Em. She liked that. "This coffee smells wonderful, too." As she sat in a chair, she answered Betsy's question. "I slept like the proverbial log. I didn't move all night, which was good. But when I woke up, I forgot about my injuries. I tried to sit up and was quickly reminded, in case you heard me yelp." Emily made a pained face and continued. "So, I lay back down and breathed through the pain, then did a very slow roll to ease off of the bed. I suspect I won't be offering to shovel snow for you or bring in firewood. I'll be happy just to make it to the bathroom in time." Betsy laughed as Emily did her best to only smile. It was obvious she was still in a lot of pain.

"All I want you to do today, young lady, is rest. The couch is waiting for you, as is Lady. I found her by your door when I got up this morning." They both looked at the dog that had rested her head on Emily's foot.

"That's where she was when I went to bed last night. I guess she knows the weakest one in the herd needs her protection," Emily said, as she reached down, in spite of her bruised ribs, to rub Lady's ear.

"Border collies are like that. She's very intuitive and sensitive to the emotions of the people around her. I guess she considers you part of her pack now," Betsy said, as both ladies smiled and looked at the black and white guardian. "I'm sure she knows by your movements that you're injured and require more attention. She'd take on a bear to protect you," Betsy said, as she put several more pancakes on a platter.

"Oh my gosh, this is going to be the best breakfast ever," Emily said, as she eyed the hotcakes. "I haven't had this kind of food in months. I sure hope you made more for everyone else. I'm on the 'see' food diet this morning," Emily opened her eyes wide at the food and grinned. Betsy giggled.

"Your pajamas are exquisite, is it silk?" Betsy gently rubbed a sleeve. "And I loved the silk blouse you wore yesterday. You looked gorgeous in that suit."

"Yes, all presents from Cooper. I'm afraid, though, that I'll be terribly overdressed while here. I only packed for my stay at his parents' house, nothing I would normally wear at home." Emily furrowed her eyebrows. "I think Cooper wanted me to impress his mom."

"Well, that's not a problem, dear. I have lots of clothes to lend to you if it would make you feel more comfortable," Betsy said with a smile.

"Yes, please, I'd rather not walk around as if going to a red-carpet affair or the Met Gala," Emily said, with a smile and a bit of sarcasm.

"I don't know, perhaps Gertrude would appreciate more class during her morning milking," Betsy snorted and laughed as Emily held her ribs and tried not to laugh.

As the women were enjoying their conversation, Andy joined them and walked to the coffee pot. He poured a mug full of the hot brew and sat at the table next to Emily.

"You ladies are having way too much fun in here without me," Andy said, as he grinned. "And I thought I better get in here before all the food was gone. I've heard rumors about your appetite, Em," Andy said, as he grinned at her.

"You must have sensed that this isn't going to last long," Emily grabbed the platter of pancakes and grinned back at him. Betsy laughed, and as Andy reached for the platter, she pretended to fight him off with her egg turner and caused them all to laugh. As Emily set the platter down, she grabbed her chest as she couldn't stop laughing.

"Ow, ow, ow!" she cried. "I didn't know laughing could be so painful." They looked at her, paused for a moment, and started to laugh again at Betsy's weapon of choice.

Cooper had come down the stairs unnoticed and wondered what had happened. The three at the table quieted down as he walked in.

"Wow, it sounded like a day at the races in here when the horses cross the finish line," Cooper said, with half a smile.

Emily, Andy and Betsy looked at each other and broke into laughter once more. Cooper didn't know why what he said was so funny. Betsy handed him a cup as she wiped her tears away. Emily noticed Betsy's tears and felt a tug at her heart. The cheerful group finally calmed down and they explained what had happened earlier, but Cooper didn't seem to be amused. He simply looked at them and then at Emily for more explanation.

"I guess you had to be here, Coop," Andy said, as he smirked. Cooper glared at the back of Andy's head, but said nothing.

"Okay, let's sit down and get to the business of breakfast," Betsy said. She reached out her hands, as did the others, and thanked God for the food and company. Cooper's face reflected that his morning already had not gone so well.

As they ate and had lively discussions about living on a mountain, the pros and cons, Cooper said very little and ate just as much. He needed to get back upstairs and make more calls, business needed to be taken care of. Being here with these people wasn't profitable.

"If you'll excuse me, I have things that need my attention." And with that he went back to his room. The others at the table seemed to feel less restricted and much more at ease again. Emily sighed and felt a bit embarrassed by Cooper.

Emily thought she needed to apologize for Cooper's lack of interaction. "Cooper has business deals that he's working on, and according to him they're worth a fortune. And his father is also training him to become the firm's next vice president, so he has a lot on his plate right now." Emily's face flushed a bit as she spoke.

"And where do you fit in?" Andy asked, and immediately looked as if he regretted his words. "I'm so sorry that I said that. It's none of my business, please forgive me," Andy said, in a sincere voice and serious face.

"That's okay, all's forgiven. Sometimes I wonder that very thing myself, but he says it will get better with time," Emily said, but she hadn't convinced herself.

"Well, I need to go feed the animals and get my chores done. I have paperwork to attend to and I'll call Dr. Michaels this morning and tell him about your injuries," said Betsy. She stood to carry some plates to the sink, and saw Lady on the floor beside Emily's feet. "And my advice to you, Emily, is for you and your dog to go lie down in the living room and rest." Betsy grinned. "It's a great place to take a nap. The sound of the burning logs puts me to sleep every time and I can see the pain on your face, dear." Betsy smiled, one that felt to Emily like a warm embrace.

"Yes, now that I'm filled by that terrific breakfast, it would be good to relax in a prone position. Things are still really sore, and I do believe my dog could use a nap, too," Emily smiled at Betsy. "I couldn't have asked for a better nurse than you, thank you."

"Of course. Now follow what I prescribed for you to get better and be a good patient. When I get this cleaned up, I'll bring you a cup of tea. The same as yesterday or some Earl Grey?" Betsy said. "But I suspect you and Lady will be napping by then."

"Earl, please. You are the best, Betsy, and you just may be right," Emily said, as she yawned and smiled.

Andy had finished the last pancake on his plate and pushed his chair away from the table. "Mom, as always, best meal ever. My compliments to the cook." Andy grinned and carried some plates to the sink. "I need to make some calls, but I'd be happy to feed the critters, if that helps you," he said, as he kissed his mom on the cheek.

"Thanks, but I enjoy talking to my friends out there. I went out early, when it was still dark, and milked the cow and goats, so that much is finished. And it will give me a chance see how much snow fell overnight. It's a good thing I wore my high-top boots my first trip to the barn. I just looked out of the window and it's still coming down pretty hard. I wouldn't be surprised if we get three feet of that white stuff before the storm passes. We're overdue for a really big one," Betsy said.

"Okay, but I'll give the path a quick pass with the shovel before you go out again." Andy turned and saw Emily struggle to push her chair back. Her face showed just how much pain she was in. She had masked it pretty well while they ate.

"Wait," Andy said to her. "Let me help you with that chair, they don't push very easily." Andy hurried behind Emily's chair and pulled it out slowly, as not to jostle her. "Here, give me your arms." He gently helped her up, but he could see it was difficult for her to stand straight. "Lean on me, Em, and we'll get to the living room together, okay?" Emily smiled up at him, appreciative for the concern and care. Andy walked her to the couch as Lady followed. He helped her to get into a comfortable position on the plush couch and propped a pillow behind her back. As he covered her with a soft throw blanket, he tucked it in to keep her warm. He smiled down at her. "Is that good?" he asked.

"Yes, that's perfect, thank you. I didn't know pain could be so exhausting. I do feel like I could nap. But I feel like a sloth," she grinned. "Even my brain is in slow motion."

"Well, there is absolutely nothing you should do except listen to your body and let it heal. If you need something, just ask me or mom, okay?" Emily nodded and felt her eyes get heavy. As soon as Andy moved, Lady took her position beside the newest member of her extended family. She gently pushed Emily's hand with her nose.

"Lady, you are my newest best friend, thank you." Emily stroked the dog's head and began to look at the Christmas tree. It was glorious, the star on top radiated and glowed. Her eyes closed and she fell asleep. Lady lay down beside her and closed her eyes, too, but was ever alert to danger.

*B*etsy called Dr. Michaels to discuss Emily. "From what you say, Betsy, I'm sure your diagnosis is right. Are the non-script pain pills helping? She's young and her body should improve pretty quickly, enough to eliminate the most severe pain at least. Sleep is the most important part of her healing, so make her stay down and rest. I'll start a chart on her here in my office and enter her into the database. If any new symptoms show up, or get worse, give me a call. Not sure what I could do in this storm, though. Thanks, Betsy, I don't know how we'd all make it without you. Take care and stay safe my friend."

"Thanks, doc. You stay safe, too. I'll call if she worsens, but I don't expect her to. I appreciate you. Bye," Betsy said, as she put the phone down. She walked in to check on Emily who was asleep. "Good girl, Lady. You keep a watch over her while I go feed the hungry crowd in the barn." Betsy leaned down and gave Lady's ear a loving rub. Lady lifted her head, looked her in the eyes and then settled in again. Betsy checked the logs in the fireplace then walked to the window and saw that Andy had cleared the path to the barn. "I better hurry before that snow gets deep again," she said out loud to herself. She put on her coat and all she needed to keep her warm, then headed out the door.

Betsy was surprised to find her son in the barn talking to Hank's horse, Max. He turned and as she walked in, they exchanged warm smiles.

"Max is a great horse. Dad did a fine job training him," Andy said.

"Yes, he did. Your dad was a man of many talents. He was so thrilled when Floyd showed up pulling that trailer. Floyd said he'd give your dad a horse for all the work he'd helped him with around his place. But he thought Floyd was just kidding, you know Floyd." They both shook their heads. "You should have seen your dad's face, he looked like a kid about to open his Christmas presents." They both laughed. Andy had heard this story dozens of times, but he never tired of it.

"I think I need to start giving him a little more feed, it's going to get colder in the next few months and he needs that fat layer to stay warm. He's such a gentle guy, just like your dad," Betsy said. As she rubbed the horse's neck, Andy saw her eyes well up.

"I miss him every day too, Mom." Andy wrapped his arm around her. "I needed to talk to Max. It makes me feel closer to dad somehow and he certainly likes the attention." Betsy gave the bay gelding a carrot she had grabbed from the bucket by the haystack. Max chomped on it while they stroked him.

Betsy laughed as she wiped her tears. "Who wouldn't like all this attention?" Andy laughed with her and squeezed her shoulders a little more.

"I'm so glad you're my mom. I don't know what I'd do without you." Andy looked down at her and said, "I love you, Mom."

"I love you too, son. And now that you're here you can help me feed everyone. I came out early this morning and milked the girls, so that's been taken care of already." Betsy grabbed a bucket and handed it to Andy. In forty minutes, they had all the animals fed and taken care of.

"Did you talk to the doc about Emily?" Andy said, as they left the barn.

"Yes, I did, and he thinks my diagnosis is spot on. I'm to call him if she doesn't improve or feels worse. We just need to keep her down and resting. And I think she, also, needs some spoiling," Betsy said. "We can take shifts." They both laughed.

"Well, I need to check in with Ben and let him know about Cooper's car on the road. Nothing can be done right now, nor needs to be, but I'll get it towed to Parsons ASAP. I just need to make sure the snow truck doesn't hit it. I'd hate for the truck to get damaged." Andy laughed at his own sense of humor. His mom playfully hit his arm.

"You're so bad, Andy. Cooper's just—misunderstood." Now it was Betsy's turn to laugh. They both knew what the other meant, they just didn't care much for Coop. Emily on the other hand was a breath of fresh air and just what they unknowingly needed in their lives.

10

Cooper made some calls to clients who were unhappy about his absence. They needed to be reminded often about how important they were, just like he did. His expensive lifestyle brought him much admiration which rewarded his efforts—and his ego. He knew someday he would be a very influential and powerful man and he needed just the right woman beside him. He decided several months ago that woman would be Emily. She wasn't as refined as he would have liked, but she was a quick learner. And in no time, he was sure, she could master the social skills she would need to be in his world. Although she didn't have the usual pedigree, he had convinced his father Emily was the right choice and she would be an asset with her law degree. His mother, however, proved to be more difficult. She had not yet gotten over Charlotte's decision to call off their wedding, although it was nearly two years ago. At the time, his mother had insisted she would handle all the preparations, as Charlotte's mother had become quite ill. Mrs. Hamilton had already made all the arrangements, sent out the invitations and paid all deposits, when she got the news of the wedding's cancellation. His mother had been distraught for weeks thereafter.

Cooper wasn't sure if it was losing a daughter-in-law that had so devastated her or losing her deposits. Not to mention losing face among her wealthy peers. In any case, his mother went on a six-month cruise with some close friends to recuperate.

Cooper put down his phone and listened; it was quiet downstairs. He thought, perhaps, he should check on Emily. He saw no one from the bottom stair so he walked toward her bedroom but, when he glanced at the living room, he saw she was asleep on the couch. As he walked toward her, Lady stood up and faced him. He could hear a low growl from the dog's chest. She definitely got her message across. He decided Emily was all right and proceeded back up the stairs. He never cared for animals and apparently the feeling was mutual.

In the last twenty-four hours, Cooper began to see that perhaps he had not spent as much time with Emily as she required. He would have to schedule her into his already full calendar. He'd hoped her work and studies would have occupied her time enough, so his absence wasn't as apparent. And he had bought a few expensive gifts for her, as his father had suggested. She seemed happy at the time to have received them, but what she needed was more of him. He didn't remember that his mother needed much of his father's attention. In fact, they had always gone on separate vacations and their hobbies and interests were not the same. His father once told him that their marriage had been a perfect arrangement. Cooper would think about this situation again—soon. For now, he had more pressing issues to attend to. He couldn't afford to lose any more sales or Mr. Hamilton would be very disappointed in him.

s Emily's eyes opened and as she moved to stretch, she suddenly stopped. The pain was a harsh reminder of what had happened to her body. She groaned and Lady stood to look her in the face. Surprised and concerned by the sound, Lady whined.

"It's okay, girl. I just need to not move so fast." Emily rubbed Lady's ear as the dog sat, her head rested on the couch. "You're just the best, Lady. I wish I could take you home with me." Lady cocked her head to one side and Emily smiled. "Do you understand me? I wish you could talk; I know we'd have a great conversation. You could tell me all about life here at Betsy's B&B." Just then, Betsy walked in the door and stomped the snow off her boots in the entryway.

"Did I hear my name?" Betsy said. "Is Lady telling stories again?" Betsy smiled at the two across the room. "Have you been awake long, Em?"

"No, maybe only about ten minutes. I had a good nap, but I'm sore and, unfortunately, I'm feeling like a turtle that can't get up. Could you help me, please? Lady's great company but lacks the skills to grab my hands. It's that opposable thumbs thing, you know," Emily grinned but was careful not to laugh. "I really need to use the restroom. And, now I know where Andy gets that habit of asking lots of questions in one breath."

"Yes, he is his mother's son—guilty as charged." Betsy chuckled, walked to the couch and gave Lady a couple pats on her head. "You're such a good girl. This is a comfortable couch but it's something of a marshmallow to get out of even when you aren't injured. Okay, Em, let's get you up." In one slow movement, Emily was up and on her feet, but held her arms across her chest to brace her ribs.

She smiled and said, "It only hurts when I breathe." Lady had moved out of the way but now she stood at Emily's side again and looked up at her.

"I have the best care ever here. Thank you. But could we move, as soon as possible, in the direction of the bathroom, please." Emily's smile reflected the urgency.

Betsy laughed. "Of course. Come on, Lady, let's get our guest to her destination."

Once Emily started to move a bit, she could feel her body loosen up and she was able to maneuver on her own. Betsy went into the kitchen to fix tea and Lady lay outside the bathroom door. Emily looked in the mirror and was shocked by what she saw. There were now several large, purple bruises across her face and forehead. She pulled down the neckline of her shirt and found more on her chest and shoulder area. "No wonder I need something for the pain," she exclaimed to her reflection.

"Are you okay, Em? Do you need some help?" Betsy called out.

"No, I'm good. I scared myself when I looked in the mirror. I'm headed in your direction now, complete with my escort." Lady looked up as Emily spoke, then looked ahead to keep her proper distance.

"Maybe we can sit by the fire and have a cup of tea. The large chairs should be comfortable for you and easier to exit. I'll bring you some water, also, and your pain pills."

"All of that sounds perfect and at the rate I'm walking I should be there tomorrow."

Betsy giggled from the kitchen and within a couple of minutes she appeared with a loaded tray. Emily had just managed to seat herself in a chair that was about eight feet from the fireplace. It was a spacious room and yet the furniture was arranged to give a sense of intimacy while people visited.

"I brought what I told you and added some of my famous tea cookies. I think you'll like them, but first something for your pain. And then treats."

Emily grinned at the way Betsy told her when she could

have her cookies. Her mom had bribed her, too. Betsy was much like her mom and it was comforting. As she swallowed her pills, she suddenly remembered Sally—she hadn't called her. Emily almost panicked.

"What's wrong," Betsy said with a concerned look.

"I totally forgot to let my sister, Sally, know what was going on. She'll be worried crazy. Would you, please, get my purse for me? It's on the floor by my bed. My brain is just not functioning properly."

"Don't worry, dear, I'll get it, and everything will be okay. Just let her know you're safe and being lovingly cared for." Betsy smiled that warm smile of hers Emily had become so fond of. "Just take a deep, slow breath and a sip of tea. I'll be right back with your purse." Emily did as she was told and calmed down in just a few breaths and a sip.

Betsy came right back with Emily's purse and as she handed it to her, Betsy heard the familiar, muted sound of the bell and smiled. "I'll be back in a few minutes, Em. I should check my phone messages."

"Okay, thanks, Betsy," Emily said, as she pulled her phone from her purse. She saw the tissue wrapped bell but grabbed her phone instead. She had a lot of missed calls and texts but had just enough battery life for a quick call to Sally.

"Hi, Sally. Before you go all ballistic on me let me explain," Emily pleaded.

"You better have a very good reason for zero communications since yesterday morning," Sally huffed.

Emily told Sally the entire story and was somewhat in disbelief herself. But Sally calmed down and was thankful her sister hadn't been more seriously hurt and was amazed at where Emily ended up.

"So, tell me, just how handsome is this stranger with the baritone voice?" Sally giggled. "And what is Cooper doing to take care of you? Don't tell me, let's see, he's on his phone, right?" Sally said sarcastically. "The one and only time I've been around Cooper was at the dinner you arranged, and he actually left the table twice to take calls. I felt it was rude at the time but he is good looking and rich. Somehow, though, in this situation I think he should be more into taking care of you. Oh, well, there are always compromises and it isn't up to me who you chose to be with."

"I'm being well cared for, Sally, so don't be concerned, okay? Hey, my battery is getting low, but I knew you'd be worried. I've just been kind of rattled about all of this. I'm safe, in good hands and I've gotten the best treatment, beyond expectations, in fact. I'm going to say goodbye before my tea gets too cold. I love you and I'll check in with you tomorrow. Bye."

"Okay, Em, but send me a photo of your knight in shining armor, please. And let me know if he's available." Sally snickered. "Take care of yourself and do what the doctor says. Love you, too, bye."

Emily smiled as she put her phone down and picked up her tea. It was just right to dunk a cookie in. It amused her how Sally had described Andy. That's what she had thought, also.

"I see you like to dunk, too," Betsy said, as she smiled and sat down. "So, I bet your sister was very happy to hear from you."

"I had the only excuse that would prevent a thrashing from her," Emily grinned at Betsy. "She was really worried about me but feels better now. We both still suffer from the anxiety of losing each other, after having lost our parents." Emily surprised herself when she shared that with Betsy. She hadn't said that out loud to anyone, not even her counselor. She'd had the passing thought about how devastated Sally would have been if she had lost her sister, too. Emily shook her head to erase that from her mind.

"Are you okay, Em?" Betsy said, as she reached over and put her hand on Emily's knee.

"I'm not sure, Betsy." Emily struggled with the tears but lost the battle. Betsy took her cup and put it down as she sat on the arm of Emily's chair and wrapped her arms around her.

"Go ahead, Emily. You need to let it out," Betsy said, as she gently rocked her. "It's going to be okay—you'll see."

11

*A*ndy sat down at his desk and saw that Ben had called twice. "Hey, Sheriff, how's it going? You have everything handled with this storm?"

"Hi, Andy, thanks for calling back. Just checking in with you to make sure you and your mom are all hunkered in and gonna be able to weather this out okay. I know she's a great party planner, but I needed confirmation," Sheriff Ben said and laughed.

"Well, Ben, as a matter of fact, this is not your typical run-of-the-mill snowstorm party we have going on here. Yesterday, on my way home, I came upon a BMW headfirst into a snowbank. There were two passengers, male and female, she had some moderate upper body pain from the airbag, but nothing broken and he's okay. He was driving too fast when a deer jumped out and, don't you know, it was at the usual deer crossing. It gets them every time. The car is wrecked, couldn't drive it even if I'd pulled it out. So, I left it there for Jerry to pick up with his tow truck as soon as this weather permits. I loaded them up in my Bronco and brought them home with me. They're city folks no doubt, he's early thirties and she's late twenties and they go by Cooper and Emily. I don't have last names on them yet but from the looks of him, he's probably missed a dinner with the governor." Andy laughed at his own joke and the sheriff joined in.

"Sounds like you've got him pretty well pegged. And I'm sure your mom is taking good care of the young woman, Emily. So, nothing you need from my end?"

"No, Mom's got it handled as always. We could survive for a couple months easy the way she handles emergency supplies and inventory. You know her. And she's happy as a clam with her unexpected guests."

"Yes, I do know her well. She's taken care of more people than I can count. That woman has the heart of an angel. This community owes her a debt of gratitude. Some day we should have a parade in her honor," Sheriff Ben said, as he chuckled.

"That would surprise her, wouldn't it? And embarrass her silly." Andy laughed hard.

"Yeah, I'd love to see that, your mom has always been unflappable. She has the best poker face of anyone I know and that's why I'd never sit in on a game with her. That is if she ever decided to play." Both men laughed. "Yeah, she's a force to be reckoned with, but a very sweet force. Okay, Andy, let me know if you need anything. Tell your mom that I sent my love and give her a kiss on the cheek for me," the sheriff said.

"My mom's a keeper for sure. Okay, Sheriff, I will. And you take it easy, too. Call me if there's something you need my help with. Bye now."

Andy always enjoyed his talks with Ben. He'd been part of his life as far back as he could remember. He and his dad had been best friends for decades. In fact, the sheriff had been his dad's best man at his parents' wedding. And Ben had been just as broken up as he and his mom when his dad died. They all shared equally in the loss and their grief made them grow even closer.

*E*mily cried in Betsy's arms until there were no more tears and her sadness had passed. All the while Betsy had comforted her, not with words, but with her spirit of love. Betsy suggested she take a long, hot bath to help soothe her aches and pains. As Emily slipped into the water, she felt the pain in her body, and her heart, melt away. It was amazing to her how easy it was to bare her soul to Betsy. She was one of those rare people you instantly trust, you know she won't judge you in any way. Her empathy and warmth allowed others to be comfortable when around her. Emily sighed; she felt a peace she had not felt in a long time.

After her bath, Emily applied the arnica cream Betsy had given her to help heal her bruises. She studied her reflection in the mirror and remembered Cooper. She hadn't seen him since breakfast but that didn't surprise her. She knew he was really stressed about being stuck here and not being at Hamilton House. Hamilton House, the name was so pretentious she refused to call it that out loud. She got dressed and when she opened the bathroom door, Lady had waited. "Yep, you're definitely coming to live with me. I won't know what to do without you, sweet girl." Lady was by her side as Emily walked to the kitchen.

"I'm back for my cookies now," Emily said as she sat at the table and grinned. Lady sat down next to her and perked her ears when she heard the word 'cookie'.

"Well, I heated your tea to just the right temperature for dunking, my dear." Betsy put the tray on the table and handed Emily her cup. "You look much more relaxed, Em. Did you use the arnica?"

As they both reached for a cookie, Emily replied. "Yes, I did, thank you. And I do feel much better, in spite of how I look." Emily dunked her cookie and took a bite. "Oh my, this is absolutely delicious." Emily closed her eyes and savored the delectable delight.

"You look beautiful, Em, and quite stunning in blue and purple." Emily was confused, she hadn't worn those colors. She then realized what Betsy meant and both women giggled and enjoyed each other's company—and the cookies.

Cooper had just completed another call when he heard the ladies laughter downstairs. He hadn't taken a break since breakfast. When he walked into the kitchen he was warmly greeted by Emily and Betsy and he smiled. It was an entirely different world down there and he seemed glad for the change of pace. But as he started to sit down, he heard a low growl, so he sat on the other side.

"Hi, Cooper," the women said in unison, each with a cookie in their hand.

"I heard you down here, Emily, and wanted to check on you." Cooper leaned over and kissed her on the cheek. "Not to mention my stomach reminded me I hadn't eaten much this morning at breakfast. Hey, those cookies look pretty good."

"Would you like some tea, or perhaps coffee? I also have milk, juice and water," Betsy said, as she stood.

"Tea would be fine, thank you." Cooper turned to Emily and saw how bruised her face was. His face grew concerned as he put his hand on hers. "That looks really painful, Emily. Is your body just as badly bruised?"

"I'm afraid so. If I just don't move much or too quickly, it's manageable enough. With some pain medicine, hot baths—and cookies—I'll be okay. Betsy's taking splendid care of me." Emily emphasized Betsy's name in an even, slow voice and Cooper's eyes widened.

"You're such a trooper, Emily. Again, I am so very sorry for what happened."

"I know, Cooper, but I wish you had just listened to me." Emily felt the anger rise in her already bruised chest. "We're lucky it wasn't any worse. You know how icy roads scare me." Emily stared into Cooper's eyes with a hint of contempt. She had never looked at him that way before.

"Yes, and I'll do better in the future." Cooper looked surprised by Emily's words and tone, as if he sensed his actions and absence had angered Emily. He didn't react to her aggravation, perhaps it was not the time nor the place to discuss anything further.

Betsy felt the tension as she set a cup of tea down in front of Cooper. "I hope it's to your liking. There's cream and sugar on the tray and help yourself to these cookies. They are quite good if I say so myself." Betsy grinned as she pushed the plate closer to Cooper and the mood at the table lightened.

Emily smiled at Betsy. "These are very good. Recipe?" Emily giggled.

"Of course, dear. I'm so glad you like them." Betsy noticed Cooper had taken a bite as she turned to look at him. "What's your verdict? Thumbs up or thumbs down?"

Cooper was chewing, but he smiled and gave a two-thumbs-up sign. Both women smiled back at him. With Emily's good humor back in place, he seemed to be in a much better disposition than earlier. In fact, the best since he'd arrived at Betsy's B&B.

The three visited for a little while before Andy walked in. The two men exchanged glances and said nothing. Andy smiled at Emily and turned to Betsy.

"Hi, Mom. Just checking if there's anything you need me to do for you."

As Andy poured a cup of coffee, Cooper stood. "Excuse me ladies, I have more calls to make. Thank you, Betsy, for your hospitality and the great cookies."

"You're welcome, Cooper. Please, feel free to help yourself to anything in the kitchen whenever you're hungry or thirsty."

"I will, thank you." Cooper gave Emily a quick kiss and

left the room. He saw the dog beneath the table and wasted no time in his departure.

Betsy turned to Andy as he sat down. "I don't think so, son, everything is pretty well situated and under control, I think. I'm just visiting with our guests."

"Okay. I thought I'd grab a coffee and a couple of these cookies." Andy turned and stared at Emily and winked. "No offense, Emily, but do you feel as bad as you look?" Andy grinned a crooked smile and laughed.

Both women laughed out loud. Emily groaned and almost spit her cookie out.

"You really know how to compliment a woman, sir," Emily said with a grin. "In fact, I just might feel worse than I look. But your mom said that these colors look quite good on me." Emily leaned her face toward Andy.

Andy laughed and turned to Betsy. "You're right, mom, those colors are perfect for her complexion." He looked at Emily and continued. "No, really. How are you?" This time Andy's expression showed deep concern.

"Let's just say it'll take a few more days before I can say I feel better. In the meantime hot baths are a true blessing. And, of course, your mom's company."

Andy smiled and looked at Betsy. "Yes, she has that effect on everyone. Which reminds me, I spoke with our dear Sheriff Ben this morning. He left a couple messages for me yesterday that I'd missed while I was busy rescuing people." Andy grinned at Emily. "He was just making sure we, especially you, were doing okay in this storm. I told him you had it handled. And he requested I kiss your cheek for him." This time Andy grinned at his mom.

"Ben's always there, he's such a good friend. Don't know how I could have managed without him the last few years." Betsy sighed. "I'll give him a call tomorrow, that's usually the day he comes out to visit." Betsy had a sweet smile on her face reserved for those closest to her heart. "Coincidentally, the same day that I make cinnamon rolls." Betsy laughed and made the other two smile. It was obvious there was a genuine feeling of affection and love between them.

"Well, thanks for the snack, Mom. I'm going to check on the animals again, and the other buildings, just to make sure everything's secure, the wind has really picked up out there with some mighty hefty gusts." He kissed Betsy's cheek. "That's from the sheriff," he said. He and Emily grinned. "Oh, I'm also going to call Angela later." Emily's smile faded.

"Be sure to give her my love," Betsy said.

"I'll see you later, Em," Andy said, and smiled at her.

"Okay," Emily replied, but there was no smile as she looked down.

Andy turned and left the room. Emily heard the front door close and she felt sad again.

"I think I'll take a nap. Thank you, Betsy." Emily struggled to get up but managed to before Betsy reached her.

"Next time let me help you, dear. There's no reason not to ask for help. Be sure to take your pain pills and have a good rest. Do you need anything else?" Betsy asked.

"No, I'm good. I just suddenly feel very tired." Lady accompanied Emily to her room and as Emily closed her door, Lady lay down at her post. "Good girl. Good to know you're protecting me." Emily carefully positioned herself on the bed and pulled the comforter over her body. She didn't quite understand her disappointment. She had probably imagined the looks she and Andy had shared, she only just met him, and she really knew very little about Andy. Besides, she was with Cooper, that's who she came with and who she'd leave with. But Emily wondered who Angela was as she fell asleep.

12

*B*etsy checked her messages and email, and her work at the desk was complete for the day. She picked up her tea and walked to her favorite chair. She sat in front of the fireplace and watched as the flames flickered around the wood. She loved this time of year. The weather forced you to slow down and reflect on where you'd been, what you were doing, and where you needed to go. Her heart felt sad for Emily, but she knew, from her own experience, that Emily's heart would not continue to be so heavily burdened. The pain never goes away completely because it shares that same space with the good memories, the happiest moments with your loved ones. That's the nature of love. With the pain comes sweet memories and with the sweet memories comes pain. But in time, love surfaces again and breathes life back into the broken heart. Betsy sipped her tea and smiled. She looked around and could see Hank in every part of the house that she could see from her chair. She remembered how hard they worked to hand pick and carry all the rocks for the fireplace. Hank often said, "I'd do anything to make you happy, Betsy. This house doesn't even begin to show how much I love you." They worked side by side, as they had all of their years of marriage, as it should be. She considered herself to have been the most fortunate woman in the world. And she knew how Hank had felt about her, because he showed her—every day. Betsy looked at the Christmas tree and took a deep breath; she loved the smell of pine. The lights twinkled and glistened on the ornaments. She got up and turned on some music and returned to her chair. She relaxed to the soft strains of angel voices, the warmth of the fire and her memories. She soon fell asleep, a smile on her face.

*C*ooper returned to his room disgruntled by his recent trip to the kitchen. He had apologized to Emily, but she seemed reluctant to actually forgive him. It had, after all, been an accident caused by a random deer. He could have driven slower, but he doubted the outcome would have been any different. He regretted she was injured, but she would entirely recover. Besides, had Emily been on time when he picked her up at her apartment, chances are they would have missed the stalled traffic and he would be talking to his father in person, rather than on the phone. Cooper paced for a few more minutes until he calmed down. He had not taken the time to notice what sorts of things had been hung on the walls in his room, he'd been too busy with the business of making money. He walked to what appeared to be a framed quote in calligraphy. He read what it said. "One of God's greatest gifts, is that of patience." He read it again and it annoyed him just as much the second time as it had the first. He had just about run out of patience. He didn't like being confined to this Godforsaken house out in the Godforsaken country. How could he be expected to run his business at peak performance stranded in the middle of nowhere? Cooper paced again more slowly until he felt his blood pressure lower. He grabbed his phone and called his office. It always made him feel better to tell other people what to do, just like any good commander.

*A*ndy had planned to call Angela, but he looked out the window and decided he should clear some of the paths around the house. It would be easier to do it now than to wait and let it build up. He got the snowblower from the shop and started it up. The snow had already accumulated quite a bit, and more was expected in the next two days at least, possibly even longer according to Ben. He realized the thought of the road closure made him happy. It meant he could spend more time with Emily. She was funny and able to laugh at herself and he found that very charming. Most of the women he'd met would have been insulted by the comment he made to Emily earlier. But she had laughed and thrown his words right back at him. That made him smile as he blew the snow off the walkways. He had met many beautiful women, but he suspected Emily was not only gorgeous but highly intelligent. And the first woman that he felt that spark with since he'd returned home. There just hadn't been any interest —until now. As he plowed through the snow, he recognized he needed to pull back or it would be difficult when she left. But when he looked into her eyes, he didn't want to leave them. But there was that minor detail of her boyfriend, Cooper. He totally didn't understand that relationship, she was so much better than that fast talking, slick looking, rich boy. As far as he could tell, money was about all that pretty boy had besides a bad disposition. And Andy just couldn't imagine it was the money that attracted Emily to him. Oh well, they'd be gone soon back to their city life and he would file her in the history section of his memory.

Andy spent an hour clearing snow from around the house

and the barn before he went in and grabbed his truck keys. It was quiet in the house except for the muted sound of Cooper's voice upstairs. He needed to move the Bronco so the parking area could be cleared, too. As he turned to leave, he saw that Emily was seated in the living room and had watched him come in. He stopped and smiled at her. She smiled back and that warmed his heart. Maybe this was a battle he needed to fight.

*E*mily's nap had been short but restful. She had lain there for a while and contemplated her relationship with Cooper. In just the past two days she realized she wouldn't want to be stranded on an island with him. She had been patient with his many missed dates due to business, but it seemed to be getting worse. He had promised months ago it would get better. Her mother had told her often that patience was a virtue, but how virtuous did she have to be when it came to Cooper? She really had thought that she wanted this relationship but being here had begun to make her reevaluate. The truth was she was thrilled not to be with Cooper's parents, she had always felt like an outsider. And the harder she tried to please his mom, the worse it got. She embarrassed herself so many times, especially at the dinner table. Mrs. Hamilton seemed to just wait for her to make an etiquette mistake. That made her nervous and invariably she would spill something. When Emily tried to say something nice once to the wait staff, she was later scolded. She had been raised to be nice to everyone, employees included; she herself was an employee. That didn't seem to sit well with Cooper's mother. No well-bred woman of her stature had ever needed to work. Emily got the distinct feeling Mrs. Hamilton didn't think she was good enough for her son. In fact, Emily had begun to think she was too good for Cooper—and his mother. Maybe she just wasn't cut out to be a rich, socialite wife. That had never been on her radar to begin with. What she wanted to be, and always had, was a lawyer, someone who could help those without a voice. And, most importantly, she wanted a man she could walk beside, not behind. She didn't want to take vacations without her husband. In the end she guessed she needed to think some more about this. She needed to have a real discussion with herself —and Cooper.

Just as Emily noticed a framed photo of Andy on a bookshelf, he walked in the door and grabbed some keys. He turned and saw her as Lady wagged her tail but didn't leave Emily's side. Andy stopped and smiled. Their look lasted longer than usual, and they smiled at each other, a smile that lingered. She liked Andy's smile—more than she should. She made a motion to be quiet and pointed to a chair where his mom was asleep. Andy nodded and walked out to complete what he had started.

13

*B*etsy was busy cooking dinner when Andy walked in to see what smelled so good.

"Mom, I think you must be the best cook in the world. You made me into this tall, strong, handsome man standing here before you." Andy wore a t-shirt and posed several times, with flexed arms, laughed out loud and kissed his mom on the cheek.

"Well, that's what happens when you do a good job feeding and watering your kid," Betsy said, and she laughed at her joke.

"So, what's for dinner tonight? It smells amazing, as always." Andy inhaled deeply.

"Just some baked chicken, scalloped potatoes, garden beans and cornbread. Oh, and cherry chocolate cake. You know, something I just whipped up." Betsy smiled and winked. "You look so much like your father when he was young. I think of him sometimes when I see you. And you're just as good a man inside, Andy, as he was. In case I haven't told you lately—I'm very proud of you."

Andy put his arm around Betsy's shoulders. "Well, the two of you set a really high standard and example. So, I've just followed my parents' footsteps." He kissed her forehead. "Should I set the table?" As he turned toward the stack of dishes, Emily stood in the doorway smiling.

Andy looked surprised and a bit embarrassed by his posing. "Were you watching the entire time?" he grinned sheepishly.

"Yes, indeed. And I agree with your assessments—all of them," Emily said with a smile. She blushed when she realized what a bold statement that had been.

Andy winked at her and grinned. Their eyes locked for a moment, they only looked away when Betsy spoke.

"So, you heard what's on the dinner menu, sound okay?"

"Absolutely. Andy said you'd fatten me up while I was here, and he wasn't kidding." Emily reached for the chair at the table, but Andy had moved closer to her and pulled the chair out.

As Emily sat, she looked up into Andy's smiling face. "Thank you, kind sir."

"Always," he said. "I'll always be here. I promise," Andy's deep voice almost whispered.

Emily remembered he had promised a few times already. She found comfort in that.

Betsy faced the stove as she cooked, but she heard their words. They didn't see her smile.

"So, Cooper, have you been able to get your business attended to?" Betsy said, as she passed the bowl of scalloped potatoes.

"Well, let's just say I've managed to put out a couple of fires, so to speak, and closed a few deals. But I really need to get back to civilization as soon as possible," he said. "When do you think that might be?"

"I checked the NOAA site today and this storm is here for

at least two more days. And it appears there may be another one right behind it, with even more snow and wind. I'm afraid this is the once-every-hundred-years type of storm. You may as well get comfortable, it'll be a while, several more days, perhaps," Andy said, as he scooped up some green beans.

"I don't know how you can live here under these conditions," Cooper said. "I'd go crazy." He sighed as he scowled and took a bite of the savory chicken.

"I guess it's all in your priorities and what's important to you," Betsy said. "Here on this mountain we take care of each other. We know all our neighbors and even their kids' names. We're like a big family of families and when we see a need, we help. I believe that's the way it should be, the way it's meant to be. And for me, it's the most satisfying life I could live and my husband, Hank, felt the same way. When your family's bigger, the love seems bigger. That's why it works for us, being a community, rather than small islands of people in a sea of indifference."

"Well, to each his own. What's important to me is my network of people not my neighbors. And if I need something, I just make a call and use my credit cards," Cooper said indifferently before he took another bite.

Emily saw that Andy was offended by Cooper's words, especially since it was a response to Betsy.

"Well, your credit cards didn't rescue you from your wrecked car and the cold. And a phone call didn't put you at this table, in a warm house, with a delicious meal set in front of you." Andy glared at Cooper and looked as if his anger was barely contained.

"Andy," Betsy said in a firm voice. "Cooper was just being honest. And I believe his presence here is no coincidence. The way he got here makes no difference—he's our guest." Betsy looked at Cooper and smiled. "Would you like more chicken, Cooper?"

"I'm sorry, Betsy, if I offended you; it was not my inten-
tion. Sometimes I don't filter what I say. I'm just used to
speaking in a business style, which doesn't always serve me
well," Cooper said. "Your hospitality and generosity have far
exceeded any five-star hotel I've stayed in. I just want you to
know how appreciative I am of everything, and also, for
taking care of Emily."

Andy sensed this was not the time to take issue with
Cooper's arrogance and his smug attitude. He took a bite of
his potatoes, as he breathed deeply to calm himself.

"These are the best scalloped potatoes ever, Betsy. Recipe,
please." Emily smiled and winked at her. Emily glanced at
Andy and saw he had watched her wink. He gave her a little
smile and she winked at him, too.

Dinner was completed with more discussion about the
weather and small talk about the latest Parsons news. Cooper
excused himself and declined dessert.

"Come sit with me by the fire, Cooper," Emily said with
a smile.

"Not tonight, Emily, I'm expecting a phone call soon.
Goodnight, I'll see you in the morning." As Cooper leaned
over Emily, a faint growl could be heard. Lady was under the
table at Emily's feet. A quick kiss later and Cooper had
ascended the staircase.

Andy saw the disappointment on Emily's face. "Let me
help, Em," Andy said. He walked behind her, put a gentle
hand on her shoulder, then pulled the chair out. "Come on,
let's find a comfy spot in the living room." He took her hands
and helped her up. "You seem to be a little steadier this
evening, but I know you're hurting. You don't fool me with
your brave act." Andy looked down at Emily and smiled as
he seated her in a soft chair in front of the fire. "I'll be back
with your cake and tea in a few minutes, Em," Andy said, as
he backed away with a bow. Emily giggled and winced.

"Andy, you're hurting me," she said with a grin.

Andy stopped with a serious look on his face. "I would never, ever, do that, Em. I promise you."

"I know that Andy."

*A*fter Cooper had gone upstairs, he checked his electronic devices. The few texts he had could wait until tomorrow. He was caught up on his immediate work and he responded to a few emails. He took a shower and checked his phone for any missed calls. He had spoken with his mother earlier and was expecting a phone call. As he put his laptop away, his phone rang.

"Hello, Charlotte."

14

"This cake is heavenly, Betsy. Have I said that before? Everything in this house seems heavenly. I feel like I'm—home." Emily surprised herself when she spoke those words. "It's so easy to feel free to be myself here and with you both. Thank you, I really mean it. My apartment is nice, well, really just okay. But I'm not there much, it's only where I shower and sleep. After five years I still have some unpacked boxes, work and school have been my priorities. My heart's just not happy in the city since my parents died. I think my dad kept me motivated about my choice to become a lawyer. I know I'll need to make a decision soon about every aspect of my current life. For now, being a paralegal has been satisfying but I think I've been feeling overwhelmed. And with the holidays it's more emotionally difficult. But enough about me." Emily smiled at Andy as she turned toward Betsy. She held up the cake on her plate. "Recipe?" She grinned and took another bite.

"Of course," Betsy said. "Oh, I almost forgot, I set some clothes on your bed for you that might be more comfortable and warmer. Most should fit."

"Thank you, it will be a welcome relief from these old things," Emily said as she pointed to her designer clothing.

They laughed and continued to share stories by the fire for a while. Emily began to grow weary and felt a hot bath would help her aching body. Andy helped Emily to her room, with Lady in tow.

"I'm going to be lost without her," Emily said, as she looked down at Lady.

"Consider yourself adopted. She's already decided you belong to her." Andy smiled and looked at Emily. "I think we all—well, we're happy you're here. If you need no further assistance, then I'll say goodnight, Em." Andy smiled.

"Goodnight, Andy." Emily paused as she looked into his eyes and smiled. "And thank you again."

"Of course." Andy turned and walked back to the living room as Emily watched him.

"That's a very fine specimen of a man, don't you agree, Lady?" she whispered.

*A*ndy went back to the fireplace and sat next to his mom. They both sat in silence, as they watched the flames flicker and crackle around the logs. After what seemed an eternity of silence and thought, Betsy spoke.

"What are you thinking, Andy?"

"I'm thinking that I wish Emily and I had met under different circumstances. I know she's with Cooper, but—" Andy's voice trailed off.

"Yes, she has someone, and it can only be her decision for that to change. I know it's hard, but the right woman will be there when you need her, son. There will be a sign, I'm sure."

"I know you're right, Mom. But Emily is the first woman, since I've been back, that I've felt that bonding with. She's so easy to be around and I can be myself. I've wanted to share more with her, but I know she'll be gone soon; it already hurts and she's still here." Andy sighed and shook his head.

Betsy took his hand in hers. "I know that in the end, it will all work out for the best." She kissed him on the cheek. "Goodnight, Andy. I love you."

"Goodnight, Mom, love you back." Andy watched the fire until the logs were just embers. He thought about pleasant possibilities, but he knew those were only wishful thinking and unlikely dreams. Finally, he got up, sighed and went to bed.

Cooper lay in bed and ruminated about his conversation with Charlotte. Until he'd heard her voice, he thought she was entirely in his past. Now, he wasn't so sure. She had broken his heart like no other had done. He was usually the one to end relationships because it would become apparent it was his money that women loved. He could understand it would be difficult to separate him from his money, but all too soon most women became obvious in their loyalty. As long as he had a lot of money, they would be with him. Charlotte had been different. She was from a wealthy family that had given her everything and would continue to do so even after marriage. But he was blindsided by her decision to run off to Europe with a wealthy Italian businessman. Apparently, he had only wanted her for a fling, a distraction from his wife. Cooper had been happy to hear how her newfound romance had ended. It was a justice befitted to her crime against him. He had seen her once at a political affair but had been able to avoid her. According to his mother, Charlotte was desperate to apologize to him; she had called her numerous times distressed by what she had done, to Cooper and their families. She paid his mother back all the deposit monies plus interest. Charlotte said that she had been too young at the time to fully realize what Cooper offered and to understand how deep her feelings had been for him. She also had not found anyone else with whom she wanted to share her love and life. When he spoke with Charlotte, memories he thought had been long buried slowly surfaced. He had sworn he would have nothing more to do with her, he knew he would never again trust her. He felt Emily was a woman of her word, someone that would not disgrace him. A partner willing to stand behind him and commit to his future. No, she would be the stable force for his plans to proceed. His life had changed, it was much different than when Charlotte had been part of the plan. When the time was right, he'd show Emily the ring. It was an impressive diamond any woman would be proud to wear. Yes, he would propose to Emily—soon.

15

*A*s Betsy put the last omelet on the table, she sat down to join in the breakfast conversation and Cooper entered the dining room as well.

"What are you wearing, Emily?" Cooper's nose wrinkled and his face twisted in disgust.

"I'm wearing what's more appropriate, more comfortable and much warmer. Betsy loaned me some clothes. By the way, Betsy, I love this blue, flannel shirt." Emily smiled at Betsy and then turned to Cooper with a tight grin and dared him to say something more.

Cooper looked surprised but continued. "So mother is getting more anxious for us to be at Hamilton House," Cooper said. "Apparently, we've already missed some of the festivities she'd planned. She said to tell you she hopes you're feeling better. Father, of course, is working on a way to extract us as soon as the storm passes. He said, when the road is clear, he'll send someone to pick us up."

Emily felt mixed emotions about Mr. Hamilton's plan. She had almost forgotten about Hamilton House and the anxiety it caused her. She'd been spoiled by the generosity, care and warmth she'd been shown at Betsy's B&B. And in the few days she'd been with them, she had grown attached to the house and its family. It would be hard to leave but she knew it was inevitable so she needed to soak up all the hospitality and love she could while there. Betsy had quickly become a surrogate mother to her and Lady a constant companion and protector. Emily heard Lady growl at Cooper several times. She wondered what the dog knew that she didn't. Like Betsy said, dogs were intuitive. It actually amused her, she didn't let on that she knew, and she didn't scold Lady.

"So, Emily, I've never asked you, what is it that you do?" Betsy said. "I'm surprised the subject has never come up. I guess circumstances have been more than unusual."

Emily smiled and held her fork. "I'm a paralegal with a large firm; it's an amazing opportunity to work on actual cases. I've already gained invaluable experience in many areas of law. And someday I hope to become an attorney. That's been my goal since I left home after graduation." Emily beamed as she continued to eat. "This breakfast is fantastic, by the way."

"Thank you, dear. I'm always happy for people when they find that place in life intended for them. It makes them so much more content." Betsy took a bite of food, then turned to Cooper. "So, Cooper, what is all this business I hear you doing upstairs?" Betsy smiled and took another bite.

"I'm a realtor with my father's firm. I'll have my broker's license soon, too. And I'm in the process of training, for the next few years, to eventually take his position when he retires. It's something he's been working on since the day I was born, I think. He's looking forward to the time when he can devote all his attention to his stable of thoroughbreds. He's also been working a plan to someday have one of his horses win the Triple Crown, then both of his game plans will have succeeded. I haven't known any of his strategies to fail, so when he gives me advice, I listen." Cooper smiled and nodded as he took a sip of coffee.

"That's impressive and it sounds like you're on your way to filling your father's shoes," Betsy said.

"And what is it you do, Andy?" Cooper said, as he turned toward him with a slight smile.

"I spent a few years in the military but when Dad died, I returned home to help Mom with her business here. I knew it would be too much for her and I'd promised to always be here for her," Andy said, as he smiled at Betsy. "And I, also, have a part-time remote job as a consultant for a company."

"Consultant? What kind of company is it?" Cooper seemed curious; he had only seen Andy do nothing more than the hotel maintenance work.

"A security firm." It was obvious that Cooper's questions were for Emily's benefit. Andy stared at Cooper as his jaws tightened and eyes steeled. A look Emily had not seen before.

"Oh, like security for local businesses?" Cooper chided with a smirk.

"Something like that." Andy relaxed his face; he looked determined not to give Cooper any satisfaction with his line of questioning.

Emily wanted—no needed—to change the conversation.

"Betsy, what are you baking? I'm almost stuffed from this prizewinning omelet and yet I'm drooling over whatever is in that oven." Emily grinned and pointed to the stove.

"Ah, I wondered who would be the first to notice that aroma," Betsy said. "Every other Wednesday I bake cinnamon rolls. And it never fails to bring Sheriff Ben to my door. Right, Andy?" Betsy said, as she and Andy both chuckled. "I guess he can smell them baking all the way from town."

"Yep, you can set your clock to it, but he won't be able to make it through the snow this week. I bet he's thinking about you right now, Mom."

"Ha, he's thinking about the cinnamon rolls, boy, not me." Betsy got a hardy laugh from her words and Andy joined in the joke.

"*A*ndy, if you don't mind would you, please, clean up the breakfast dishes? I have some calls to return to some folks nearby," Betsy said, as she rose from the table. "No need for anyone to hurry. Besides, the main course will be finished baking in about ten minutes." Betsy laughed as she walked away.

"It's just not fair, Betsy, I'm sure I've already gained weight," Emily said, as she giggled.

"That's what I do best, dear. I'll be in my office if anyone needs me. I'll see you a little later, Em. Go rest by the fire and relax."

Cooper stood and looked down before he bent to kiss Emily. Lady watched his every move. He didn't waste any time as he walked away from the table and up the stairs. They heard Cooper close his door.

"I guess that just leaves us—with the cinnamon rolls," Andy said with his crooked grin.

"Oh, my gosh. I swear your mother is fattening me up on purpose," Emily said, as she stretched her arms out.

"You look beautiful, Em. You're perfect, in fact." Andy smiled as he stood up, plates in his hands.

Surprised by his words, Emily hesitated and said, "Thank you, kind sir." She lowered her head as if to bow.

"You stay seated and let me clean this up, Em," Andy said, as he walked to the sink, his hands loaded with plates.

"Well, I can at least clear some of this for you. But only if you'll pull my chair out for me. It's still a bit too painful to push this heavy chair out."

"Of course. How are you feeling today? You seem to be sitting a bit taller now," Andy said, as he pulled Emily's chair away from the table and helped her to stand.

"Considering I got kicked by a mule, I'd say I am doing better today. Thank you for asking, Andy. It's getting easier to get out of bed now and I'm thankful I haven't had to sneeze." She smiled, careful not to laugh. "All in all, I'm improving thanks to your mom's care and your assistance. It has been appreciated more than I can say. I'm worried, though, that I've become accustomed to taking several naps a day. That could severely interfere with my work." She grinned at Andy, who grinned back.

Andy rolled up his sleeves to load more plates onto his hands and arms. Emily saw large scars on his forearms and reached her hand out to touch them. Before Andy could turn away, he felt her fingers, and as he watched, she slowly ran her fingertips over the scars.

"How did this happen, Andy?" Emily said, her other hand now holding his arm. She seemed concerned, almost sympathetic and not repulsed, as he had expected.

"It's a reminder of my time in the military, and man's inhumanity to man."

Emily looked up at Andy and he could see a tear in her eyes and compassion on her face. "I'm so sorry that anyone has to experience that. But thank you for your sacrifice."

"Mine was nothing compared to those who didn't come back to their loved ones,." Andy said. And he felt for the first time that he had spoken about the war without the gut-wrenching pain, and the immeasurable guilt. He smiled back at Emily and placed his hand on hers for a fleeting second.

"Okay, back to the business of kitchen detail," he said, with a warm smile. "I'll clear the table, if you'll take a peek inside the oven. We wouldn't want the entree to burn," Andy said, as he chuckled.

"That I can do," Emily said, and grinned at Andy. She walked across the kitchen to the stove and opened the oven door. "Oh, my, it's official. I have gone to heaven." Emily inhaled the sweet scent of cinnamon and yeast as she closed her eyes. "I'm not sure if the rolls are done, I can't open my eyes. I'll just stand here and inhale."

"If it's all the same to you, Em, I'd rather eat my cinnamon roll, or two, maybe three. Yeah, you're right, I get it. Mom's on a mission to fatten up all of us." Andy and Emily grinned at each other.

"Okay, all those in favor of taking this pan to the table— say aye and raise your hands," Emily joked. Andy raised both hands as they laughed again.

*C*ooper checked his phone. Charlotte had called while he was downstairs and left a message.

"Hi, Cooper. Thank you so much for taking my call last night. I hope you know now how truly sorry I am. Your mother has invited our family for dinner again next week. It will be nice to see you again. Call me if you want to talk before then. Love you."

Cooper sighed as he threw his phone on the bed. He just wished he could get out of this place and be somewhere normal; he missed his morning laps in the pool. Not only did it keep him in shape, but it did wonders for his attitude. The anxiety of being cooped up here was really getting to him. His father was a constant reminder that he had made a wrong decision when he chose to take the side road. One of his sales, on a large property, was hanging in the balance. In his absence, he hoped his father could close the deal for him or at least stall the buyer.

"I can't understand why a person would live out here, so far from life in the real world," Cooper muttered. Business could wait he decided. He got in the shower and hoped the hot water might, at least, loosen his tension even if it didn't give him a workout.

Cooper's father had repeated time and again, 'Remember, before you decide anything, the results must outweigh the consequences.' The point of that hit home, Emily was the safe decision. He couldn't place his trust in Charlotte's words.

*J*ust as Betsy finished her calls, her phone rang. She smiled when she saw the caller ID.

"Well, hello there, Sheriff Murphy," Betsy said, in a cheerful voice.

"Hello, sweet Betsy. Are those cinnamon rolls I smell?"

Betsy laughed out loud. "Only if you have the nose of a bloodhound, Ben." She smiled when Ben laughed. He always knew how to brighten her day.

"I can't be there like usual, so I just called to hear your voice. Is everything good out your way? How are your unexpected guests liking your B&B? And the girl, Emily, is healing up?"

"Well, Cooper is a high-finance type of guy, pretty self-important, I think. He's been ready to leave since he got here. Emily, on the other hand, she's doing good. It'll take a little while, but she's moving around better each day. I really like her, she's a charming young woman. If you ask my son, I'm sure he'd throw in the word beautiful, too."

Ben chuckled. "So, he's enjoying the new view, eh?"

"That he is, Ben. And you know, she's been a breath of fresh air for both of us. It'll be tough to see her leave. But you never know." Betsy's voice chirped as she smiled.

"Ha, a big city girl that wants to move to Parsons? I'll dance down Main Street if that happens." Ben snickered.

"And when was the last time you went dancing, Sheriff Murphy? Our high school prom, maybe?"

They both laughed and snorted about the fun the three of them had that night.

"I danced every song that night between the two of you. I was so worn out I slept till noon the next day. That night is such a great memory, Ben. You and Hank looked so handsome in your tuxedos." Betsy sighed. "I'm thankful for every moment I spent with both of you."

"Me, too, Betsy. We were quite the trio around town, weren't we? And prom night, Hank and I were speechless when you walked down the staircase; you looked stunning in that gown. We had to close each other's mouths," Ben said, as he laughed.

"That's one of the things I love about you, Ben. I have someone to share Hank's memory with. I appreciate that."

"Me, too, and I think we were mighty lucky to have Hank in our lives."

"So, do you have any new information on weather and road conditions I need to pass along?" Betsy said.

"Let's see, we still have lots of snow coming down. And roads are still closed. That about sums it up." Ben laughed at himself. "Nope. Everyone just needs to stay home and off the roads until further notice. It may be about three or four days before we can get the machinery up your way. We have to clear town and emergency exits first. But hopefully, by Christmas, if this snow lets up, we can get your road cleared. I'll make sure to keep you posted."

"Okay, good. And tell me, how are you doing, Ben? I worry about you eating right. You put on some pounds last winter that you didn't take off this summer."

"You're the one making the sweets, Betsy," Ben admonished.

Betsy giggled at his mocked sense of being offended. "I know, I know, but it's my way of making sure you come to visit. You don't actually have to eat anything," she teased.

"You don't have to bribe me to get me there, but it helps." They both laughed for a long time. "I'll let you go, Betsy. Thanks for the laughs and call me any time. Love you. Bye."

"Same here, Ben. Take care and love you back. Bye."

As Betsy put the phone down, she looked at the clock and

Chapter 15 105

realized her sweet rolls had needed to come out minutes earlier. She hurried to the kitchen only to find Andy and Emily had each just finished a roll with their tea. They both looked at her with guilty faces. Betsy couldn't help herself as she burst out laughing and they grinned like the Cheshire Cats.

"Oh, Andy, I forgot to ask about Angela. How is she?" Betsy asked.

"I didn't call her yet, I got distracted for some reason. I'm on my way now to call her. I'll tell her you send your love," Andy said. He smiled at Emily, but her smile faded.

*A*ndy pressed the number for Angela. Memories flooded his mind. He shook his head and cleared his thoughts when he heard Angela's voice.

"Hi, Andy. You've been on my mind. How are you?" Angela asked in a loving tone.

"I'm good, Angela, really good. I've been thinking about you, too, and wanted to check on you and Christina. Oh, before I forget, my mom sends her love to you both. Hey, thanks for the pictures you sent. Christina's getting so big now and she's absolutely beautiful. I'm gonna stay busy keeping the boys away when she's older," Andy said, in a teasing tone.

"I know, she's so beautiful and she's my sunshine. Just to see her smile warms my heart. I know Willie is watching down on us and he's proud of our little girl," Angela said.

"He showed me pictures of you two every single day. And I could see how much he loved you, it was written all over his face."

"I know, Andy. Willie told me every chance he got how much he loved our little family. We miss him—a lot. But he filled our hearts with enough love to last a lifetime, you know.

Not a day goes by that I don't feel his presence and that love. And I tell baby Christina that her daddy loves her. You should see her face light up when I show her his picture. I think she knows, and if not now, someday she'll understand."

"Do you need anything, Angela? Is your car running well? Do you need any money? Did you get the Christmas box I sent?" Andy said, without taking a breath.

Angela laughed. "You're so funny, Andy. Willie told me you always asked rapid-fire questions before he could answer. No, we don't need anything. It's all good here. And we got the box, thank you. I put the gifts under the tree already. I've sent you something. Let me know when you get it, okay?" Angela said. "But what I want to know is—how are you really, Andy? How is the 'way down deep inside of you' doing? This will be the second Christmas without Willie and I know you miss him, too."

Andy wiped away his tears and smiled. "You know me too well, Angela. I'm getting better, though, just like you. I have my days but there's more time in between now. And the darkness doesn't smother me like it used to, in fact, that's pretty much gone now. I'm happy with the life here, it suits me. As long as I can help people, I'm good. It helps me feel better about myself."

"I'm so glad, Andy. I was so worried about you. But you sound like you're in a much better place. Hey, can you hear Christina? That's my five-minute warning," Angela said, as she giggled. "Merry Christmas, Andy. We love you."

"Yeah, I hear her. Kiss and hug her for me. Maybe I can come visit next year. I love you both, too. Merry Christmas, Angela." Andy grinned as he hung up. His calls were so much easier now. They had been so agonizing the first year. They needed each other, he and Angela, because the pain was almost unbearable for both of them. They agreed they both had to stay strong for Christina's sake. Andy had promised Willie he would always be part of their lives.

16

*S*heriff Ben put his phone down and sighed. He had known Betsy since fourth grade and been in love with her from the first time he saw her. At recess, she and Hank welcomed him to school and into their lives, and they'd been best friends all these years. He knew Betsy and Hank were destined for each other and he was happy to be part of their world. Ben found and married Rachel a few years after Hank and Betsy tied the knot. The four of them did everything together. But Rachel died at the young age of thirty without having had any children. Ben was devastated and leaned heavily on the love and support from his good friends. He poured his fatherly energy into Andy and gave himself to his job as the sheriff of Parsons. Over the years he developed a close kinship with many of the families in town. This was his town, these were his people and he was happy. And thankful for Betsy's friendship.

When Hank died, he shared as deeply in the loss as Betsy. She leaned on Ben for solace just as he had leaned on her and Hank when he lost Rachel. Now there was just the two of them as best friends, confidants and kindred spirits. There was nothing he wouldn't do for her.

Sheriff Murphy's office door opened and the local attorney, Leroy Gibbs, entered and stomped the snow off his boots. "Hey, Ben, you had enough snow yet?" he chided.

"Nah, I think we need about three more feet, Leroy," Ben said, and chuckled as he rubbed the stubble on his cheek.

"Lord have mercy, I'm already tired of it and winter's just started. I'm overloaded with work and having to shovel this snow is just too much. I should retire and move to Florida."

"I told you, Leroy, get one of the kids in town to keep your driveway clear. There are several boys I know that can use some money, unless, of course, you're just too cheap to hire someone." Ben leaned back in his chair and laughed.

"Okay, you call one of them for me. And I'll be happy to pay someone at this point. I don't remember this much snow before," Leroy said, as he shook snow off his hat, rubbed his bald head and adjusted his glasses.

Ben leaned forward on his desk toward the attorney. "You? In Florida? You'd melt into a puddle of legal jargon. You know you're supposed to be here. Besides, who would there be in town to yell, "Your Honor, I object!" Both men laughed out loud and Ben pounded his fist on his desk.

"I know, Ben, you're right. But with all the new people moving into Parsons, my caseload has more than doubled. It's getting hard to keep up these days and I'm getting too old to work this hard anymore." Leroy scratched his chin and shook his head.

"Well, I know you'll figure it out. That's why you're the lawyer and I'm not." Ben smiled at Leroy and asked, "How 'bout a cup of coffee? I just made it." Ben stood up and stretched.

Leroy snickered. "I don't know why some pretty woman hasn't snatched you up, Ben. You got that tall, lanky, cowboy look going for you. Me, I just get older, shorter and rounder. Oh, and don't forget balder." The two friends laughed as the sheriff ran his hand over his full head of silver hair and then whisked his finger under his mustache.

*B*etsy and Emily sat by the fire and drank their tea. The fireplace seemed to ease Emily's worries and soothed her sore muscles.

"I'm glad you're feeling a bit better, Em, but you still need a lot of rest. I spoke with the doc to give him an update and those are his orders, too." Both women smiled. "I wish I could adopt you, Em, and just keep you here, purely for selfish reasons, of course. You've been such good company for me, it's nice to have some girl talk for a change. Andy's terrific, but he only has a male perspective." Betsy lifted her eyebrows and the women giggled.

"I feel the same way, Betsy. And purely for the cinnamon rolls," Emily said, as she licked her lips. "I swear, those things are addictive." Emily beamed. "Maybe I'll just empty my suitcase and fill it with those before I leave." They giggled again, but this time Emily winced. "I guess I need to quit laughing at my own jokes, it hurts."

"Oh, by the way, you haven't ventured past this room. But if you'd like a book to read, the library is just through those large doors. Andy also uses it for his office, but he doesn't mind anyone going in there," Betsy said, and motioned toward the tall, ornate doors.

"Yes, that sounds wonderful. I haven't been napping as much when I lie down, and I'm pretty sure the extra walking would be good for me. It doesn't seem very far, but the past couple of days have really limited me to slow, short distances." Emily smiled, confident she was up to the challenge.

"I'm going out to feed my crew in the barn. They need their strokes, too. If you're up to it, maybe you'd like to visit them before you leave. We started gathering our menagerie of furry and feathered friends to give our guests a farm experience and it's been a big hit. And to watch them get excited about milking Gertrude and the goats is pure pleasure. I think Andy is clearing the driveway, so you'll have the downstairs all to yourself for now."

"Sounds good and, yes, I'd really like to meet your barn friends. I love animals of all kinds. Andy has spoken about Max and how gentle he is, so I'd especially like to give him an apple and a hug," Emily said with a smile.

"You're welcome to come along anytime, dear." Betsy gave Emily a smile and quick hug.

*A*ndy had just cleared their long driveway when he heard his phone. He'd missed several calls from Sheriff Ben. He listened to the first one then called back.

"Hi, Andy. You heard the message, right?" Ben said, his voice serious and anxious. "Sarah Meyers called about twenty minutes ago. She's worried about Caleb. He went out to cut a Christmas tree about three hours ago and hasn't returned. He told her he'd be back in about an hour. With this snow coming down, and trails covered, he may have taken a wrong turn. We need to find him. Sarah said he didn't take any food or water with him. The temperature's not extreme but he shouldn't be out there much longer. I have eight other men who can meet us at the Larson Trailhead. How soon can you meet us there?"

"I just cleared the driveway, so that will make it faster for me. I can meet you there in thirty minutes," Andy said.

"Okay, good. That's about the time the rest of the guys will be there. See you soon." And the sheriff ended the call.

Andy thought about the emergency medical bag he kept packed as he hurried to the house.

17

*B*etsy packed food, water and filled a couple thermoses with coffee. She also gave her son a duffel with a blanket, winter jacket, snow pants, extra gloves and warm hats. Andy had packed the gear on the snow machine and double checked his communications. He was ready to go within ten minutes. This had happened many times before, so the routine was second nature to them.

As Andy walked to the door Emily put her hand on his arm. Andy stopped and they exchanged smiles. "Please, be careful, Andy. I want you at the dinner table tonight."

"I will, Em," Andy said, as they continued to look into each other's eyes.

Betsy walked up to them with a small, plastic container. Inside was a sweet roll.

"Give this to the good sheriff for me," Betsy said, as she handed over the treat. "Okay, I know I don't need to tell you to be safe, Andy. But I want you to come back. Call me when you find him. And tell Ben, no heroics today. Just let the young ones take the chances." She hugged Andy and kissed him on the cheek.

"Will do, Mom, but you really know how to hurt a guy.

The sheriff won't be happy about you calling him old." Andy grinned as he walked down the stairs to his machine, pulled his goggles over his eyes and roared at top speed into the falling snow. Within seconds, he was out of sight.

"*D*oes this happen very often, Betsy?" Emily said, as the women walked into the kitchen.

"Maybe two or three times a winter. It's easy to get disoriented when everything you see is covered in snow and the snow is coming down this hard. It's also easy to get hurt. We haven't lost anyone, but living out here has its danger." Betsy poured tea into the cups and handed one to Emily. "I called Caleb's wife, Sarah, and she said she tried to talk him out of going but he insisted he didn't want to wait any longer to get a tree. He'd been sick for several days so wasn't able to go before today. Poor Sarah's worried sick." Betsy slowly shook her head. "I hope he's alright and it's just a problem with his machine; that happens often."

"Would it be okay if we sat in the library? I'd really like to see it," Emily said with a bit of excitement in her voice.

"Certainly, I think you'll like it in there. Hank was a voracious reader and a lover of travel and history. In fact, we traveled to all the continents and dozens of countries. It was a dream of his to see the world and I have so many memories of our travels together. Our last trip, before Hank got sick, was to Paris. It was marvelous as we stood on top of the Eiffel Tower. It was at night and the view of the city was breathtaking. Just before he took me in his arms and kissed me, he said, 'We'll always have Paris.' That was a line from our favorite movie, Casablanca. Hank was quite the romantic," Betsy said, with a wistful smile and a faraway look in her eyes. "I miss that man. He really knew how to treat a girl." Betsy giggled.

The women put their teacups on a table between two exquisite Victorian armchairs tufted in red velvet. The room was in the lower half of the tower on the house and its curved walls and ornate details were amazing. The large, expansive windows presented a view to the meadow below. Emily walked closer to the windows and held her breath just to stop her movement. She would have stopped her heart if she could. She wanted to remember this image always, it was beauty beyond measure. The snow had stopped momentarily, allowed the sun to peek through, and gave way to the most splendid picture of winter she had ever seen. Most likely she would not be so privileged again. She marveled at God's creation and wondrous beauty. It so inspired her spirit that a tear rolled down her cheek. Betsy smiled as she watched Emily's reaction. She, too, had felt the same many times before and thanked God, and Hank, for what she had been given.

"I have never seen anything so magnificent in all my life. And the snow sparkles like millions of diamonds or the stars in the clear, night sky. This is a piece of heaven, I'm sure," Emily said, as she turned to face Betsy. "Thank you for this beautiful memory."

"You are so very welcome, my dear. It does lend a different perspective to life, doesn't it?"

The women sat and sipped their tea in silence as Emily gazed around the room. There were hundreds of books on shelves that reached from the floor to the high ceiling. There were four other chairs arranged in cozy pairs with small tables and lamps. Off to the far side was a smaller window facing the back of the house. Below the window, between two sets of bookcases sat a large desk, Andy's desk. It was cleared except for a stained-glass table lamp, desk calendar and notepad. But on the bookcases Emily saw something intriguing that captured her attention.

"What are in those frames by the desk?" Emily asked as

she rose from her chair. Betsy stood up, also, and followed Emily toward the desk.

"Wow, these are photos of Andy in uniform. It looks like these were taken over several years. Where was he stationed?" Emily asked, as she continued to look at the pictures.

"Mostly in Afghanistan. He doesn't talk about it much anymore. He was severely injured and has some metal plates and screws holding parts of his body together. As he was healing, his father died and that's what brought him home. He would have gone again, but I'm glad he didn't. I think he's finally at peace with not being there. He felt it was personal when his best friend, Willie, was killed. It happened in a roadside bomb; Andy was injured but Willie died—in his arms. I know he blames himself for what happened but there was nothing he could have done differently, he had to follow his orders. Willie's wounds were too serious for Andy to have saved him and the helplessness he felt injured his soul." Betsy paused and sighed. "He and Willie had been friends since high school and even enlisted together. Andy was devastated by the loss of Willie and his father at almost the same time."

"That breaks my heart for him," Emily said. She looked at other frames that held medals, ribbons and letters. She started reading the inscriptions and then turned to Betsy. "He received the Medal of Honor—the Congressional Medal of Honor?" Emily said, astonishment written all over her face. "And all these other medals, and ribbons—and commendations."

"He never talks at all about these, he doesn't feel he deserved them. I begged him to let me display them, if for no other reason than I needed to preserve them for posterity. And some day his children will see his medals and understand how brave their father had been. He ran in when most others ran out," Betsy said. "I'm surprised you saw these, not many people notice them over here."

Betsy's phone rang. "Hi, Andy. What's the news? Did you find Caleb?" Betsy laughed, relieved by the call. "Okay, I'll see you in an hour and I'll have a fresh pot of coffee waiting for you. Thanks for calling. Love you, too."

"Well, that all sounded like good news," Emily said and smiled.

"Yes. They found Caleb, on foot, not far from home—dragging a Christmas tree." Betsy laughed out loud at the image Andy had described.

"He was covered in snow, cold and tired, but by golly, he had a Christmas tree for his wife. Now that's what I call love," Betsy said, as she nodded and giggled. "It seems his snow machine refused to start. And he told the guys he didn't want to leave the tree because someone might come along and steal it." Both women chuckled.

"Let's go put some lasagna in the oven for dinner." Betsy led the way as Emily followed.

*A*s the women walked into the kitchen they heard Cooper upstairs as he screamed at someone on his phone. They were surprised as they hadn't heard him lose his temper before—ever.

"I don't care what you have to do," Cooper yelled. "If that contract isn't completed by the time I get back to civilization —you're fired." He then mumbled something and went silent.

Emily's eyes were wide and filled with alarm. She looked at Betsy. "I've never heard him raise his voice before. It's not a side of him I've ever witnessed, and I don't think I like it." Emily was clearly distraught by Cooper's actions. He probably didn't think they would hear him, or he didn't care. Or perhaps, his anger had overridden his ability to remain calm. Emily sat down at the counter as Betsy worked in the kitchen.

She looked sad and confused. She fought back the tears that stung her eyes, but she lost.

After a few minutes Betsy handed Emily a tissue and set a cup of chamomile tea in front of her. "I have dinner in the oven, let's go look at the Christmas tree by the fireplace." Emily followed Betsy but said nothing. Betsy turned the angel choir music on low.

They sat in silence as Emily watched the twinkling lights on the tree and the music soothed her soul. After she gained her voice and composure she spoke. "Your Christmas tree is so beautiful. The star on top reminds me of the one on the tree at the antique store in Parsons. What's the name of it? Oh, right, Celestial Antiques. Which reminds me, you and your sister look identical. When I saw you, the day we drove up to the house, I thought I must have injured my head." Emily and Betsy laughed. "Andy assured me I wasn't hallucinating, though. Estelle was so nice and helpful and, by the way, you both are so incredibly beautiful. Well, I'd forgotten Mrs. Hamilton's gift at my apartment, so we stopped there. I found a lovely bell and your sister gave it to me. I was shocked but she insisted." Emily's eyes widened in surprise. "And I've totally forgotten about it. It's still in my purse." Emily started to get up, but Betsy put her hand on Emily's arm.

"Let me get your purse again, dear. Is it still on the floor by your bed?" Betsy said.

"Yes, thank you. I haven't really taken the time to look closely at the bell. It's even still wrapped."

Betsy returned in a matter of seconds and handed the purse to Emily. She reached inside and found the bell wrapped in tissue. As soon as Emily lifted it up, she heard a soft jingle. It made her smile, her heart felt warmer and she no longer felt sad.

"I promised Estelle I would listen several times to the bell ring before I gifted it," Emily said, then stopped with a shocked look on her face. "And that's where I first met, actually bumped into, Andy," she said. "Cooper was outside honking at me, so I didn't say much at the time and I've been so scattered I forgot to tell you. When Andy stopped to rescue us, he leaned into the car and we were both shocked at seeing one another. What a small world. And how lucky we were that he came along." Emily smiled as she recalled the events and shared them with Betsy.

Betsy laughed, and said, "Do you believe in destiny? How about some serendipity? Fate or chance? Maybe divine intervention? Whatever brought you here is my good fortune," Betsy said, with a grin and a wink.

18

*A*s Emily unwrapped the bell it jingled every now and then. The sound filled Emily's heart with joy. The anxiety of the last few days seemed to melt away. She held it up and gently moved the dainty, red bell. The sound it made blended in with the choral music and Emily was lost in a divine melody. She sighed and felt her body rejuvenated. "I think this bell has a magic spell on me," Emily said, as she smiled blissfully at Betsy. "Would you mind if I hung it on your tree, just until we leave? I'll be reminded to ring it several times."

"Of course, dear. I enjoy hearing it, too. It has such a delicate and unique sound. It's almost as if it whispers to your soul," Betsy said.

"You're right. That's a perfect way to describe the feeling." Emily hung the bell on a branch near her chair. She touched the bell again and listened to its song. Her frustration, fear and confusion were replaced with a peace and calm. The sweet-toned bell was music to her heart.

❄

*E*mily napped while Betsy finished cooking the evening meal. She was reassured by Emily's continued healing and hoped that the young woman's mind would, also, be renewed while there. It filled her with contentment and satisfaction to help nourish a person's body. While the house offered a place for her guests to rest and restore their minds and spirits, she provided the sustenance and hospitality. It was her mission and ministry in life. She had come to regard her B&B much like a hospital for the weary and faint of heart for those who were in need of respite from the heartbreak and worry that life often brought. And for those souls who stood at crossroads in their lives. She merely provided the strength and time for healing, and an opportunity for the confusion to be cleared from their minds.

Betsy heard footsteps and was surprised to see Cooper walk in. He hadn't usually appeared until dinner was on the table.

"Well, hello there, Cooper, you're early this evening. How are you?"

"Hi, Betsy. I'm fine thanks. I finished with all my business for today, so I thought perhaps I'd come down and socialize. Where is everyone?"

"I'm glad you did. Emily is sleeping and Andy went to a neighbor's today. Would you like some tea or coffee? I have both already made."

"Coffee would be great; I'll just help myself. I'm glad Emily has been resting. I don't feel so guilty not spending time with her. Dinner smells good and I have to compliment you on your cooking skills, everything I've eaten has been first rate. In fact, you could have a successful career with your own restaurant. I'd be happy to look into that for you, as a return on what you've done for Emily and me." Cooper smiled and sipped his coffee.

"Thank you for your kind words and generous offer but

my life is here, in my little bed and breakfast. It's actually very rewarding. And as I've gotten older a feeling of a job well done, no matter how seemingly insignificant, is more important to me than any fame and fortune. I don't need my name on a building, the plaques hanging on my walls are more than enough for me." Betsy smiled at Cooper and continued. "I so appreciate your offer, Cooper, it's very kind of you. And as for a return or repayment, you have no debt here. It's entirely my pleasure and gift to you both. This house allows me to live in harmony with God's plan for me."

Cooper smiled but the look on his face showed he was a bit offended. He had just made an offer, and no one had ever refused his generosity. He guessed Betsy was a person who enjoyed a small life, with little probability of wealth and security. He considered it her loss. He continued to drink his coffee in silence as he watched Betsy. He noticed a small plaque above her sink and read it out loud. "We each are given gifts. How will you use yours?" Cooper thought for a moment. "Well, my father has given me a lot of things, but the most important gift to me would be his advice on how to succeed in making money. Wealth buys not only assets but happiness, I believe."

Betsy listened carefully and she understood what Cooper really lacked. It wasn't money or riches. She wondered if he would ever understand what those words really meant and how life changing it could be for him. They hadn't heard Andy come in the front door.

"Hi, Mom," Andy said, as he walked over and kissed her on the cheek. He looked at Cooper and nodded. "Good evening, Coop. Did you sell lots of real estate today?"

"I did, actually, and made a lot of money," Cooper said with a smug look.

"That's great, good for you," Andy said, as he dismissed the other man.

"How long until dinner? Do I have enough time for a quick shower?" Andy gave his mom one of his crooked grins.

"About fifteen minutes, so make it quick." Betsy turned to Cooper. "Would you, please, wake Emily. She's napping on the couch by the fireplace."

Cooper walked in to wake Emily, and in the semi-darkness he hadn't noticed Lady. As he reached to touch Emily's arm, Lady stood and growled. It startled him and he backed away. Emily was awakened by the sound of Lady's warning. "Lady," Emily said, "no." Lady lay down again but continued to stare at Cooper. Emily slowly sat up and realized Cooper stood near her.

"I don't know why that mutt doesn't like me," Cooper snarled and glared at the dog.

"Maybe she knows you don't like her. Dogs are like that," Emily said as she gave him a weak smile.

"It's time for dinner, Emily. You have about ten minutes. I'd give you a kiss, but I don't want to be bitten."

"Lady won't bite you, I don't think. Okay, I'll freshen up and meet you at the dining table," Emily said. She was sore from having lain so long on the couch. She would have asked Cooper for assistance, but he'd left the room in a huff. She felt rested, albeit a bit uncomfortable from her bruised ribs and shoulders. She wondered if Cooper really understood how close he'd come to seriously injuring her. She felt disappointed in his lack of caring. She had, also, been embarrassed and disquieted by the way he shouted earlier. She supposed his confinement was having an emotional effect on him. She, too, felt an effect but it had been much different than his.

"*Y*ou should have seen him," Andy threw his head back and laughed. "He looked like the Abominable Snowman—dragging a Christmas tree."

Andy could barely get the words out as he laughed so hard. Betsy and Emily chuckled as they listened to Andy's account of the day's rescue.

"And we all couldn't believe he had dragged that tree, through knee-deep snow, for a couple hours, because he didn't want anyone to steal it. When Sheriff Ben stopped laughing, he wanted to know from Caleb, who in the world he thought would just happen by, out in the middle of nowhere on the side of a mountain, to steal his tree." Andy laughed even harder.

The ladies were almost in tears as they laughed at the story of Caleb and his Christmas tree. Emily several times held her arms across her chest in pain. The humor seemed to be lost on Cooper as he completed his dinner, while the others at the table had barely touched their food.

Betsy dried her tears. "Well, that's a story to share at every town meeting for years to come. But I'm thankful that Caleb's rescue had a happy ending, I know Sarah was greatly relieved when I called her." Betsy took a bite of her semi-warm food as she smiled. "I love happy endings," she said, as she smiled at Emily.

"And thanks, Mom, for packing all the extra warm gear, it came in handy. And Sheriff Ben was mighty happy you'd sent that cinnamon roll for him and he grinned as he ate it in front of everyone." Andy laughed and both women giggled.

As Cooper stood, he said, "Well, if you'll excuse me, I'm expecting a phone call soon. Have a good night everyone and enjoy yourself, Emily. I hope you feel better in the morning." Cooper turned and walked up the stairs.

Emily was hurt that Cooper hadn't kissed her. He seemed annoyed by all their laughter.

19

*B*etsy served up bowls of hot apple pie and suggested they go sit by the fire. Andy pulled up an extra armchair beside Emily. He smiled down at her and said, "Is this seat taken, fair lady?" Both women giggled.

"How are you feeling this evening, Em?" Betsy asked and smiled.

"I'm not sure, after all that laughing at the dinner table my ribs ache a little more than they did before I sat down." Emily grinned. "But it was worth it. That had to have been a sight to see, alright. That was so good how all of you went out to search for him, though. It's got to be reassuring to all who live here that there are those among you who will help."

"I was raised that way, Em," Andy said, in between bites. "There's no reason anyone should ever feel alone and unable to reach out for help, even living on a mountain."

"By the way, I've meant to ask. I saw the town sign when we drove in, but what is the name of this mountain?" Emily said, with curiosity in her eyes.

"Technically, it's called Iris Peak on the maps and in the spring the flowers are amazing." Betsy said. "But the locals all call it Glimmer Mountain. Legend has it there was a miner named Larson who got lost up here during a snowstorm while he was hunting. He was missing for two weeks, at frigid temperatures. When the storm passed the search party found him. They saw his red scarf blowing on a branch outside a small outcropping of rocks. He was curled up, covered in pine branches, in an unoccupied bear's den. He looked like death warmed over, but he was alive. He said he got lost because the snow covered the trail down the mountain. He was near frozen and had almost given up. But he remembered his wife had often told him, 'You never give up. As long as you have breath, there's a glimmer of hope.' That sustained him until he was found."

"That's an amazing story," Emily exclaimed. She had eaten all her dessert and was fully engaged in Betsy's story.

"And another detail about the story—his wife's name was Iris," Betsy said and grinned.

Emily's eyes widened and she clapped her hands. "I love that story." She smiled and looked at Betsy and Andy. "Almost as much as the two of you and apple pie." They each had a good chuckle.

*T*he three continued to share their stories and laughter by the Christmas tree and fireplace. "That tree reminds me, Andy," Betsy said, "I spoke with Aunt Estelle earlier and she told me about a few families that are struggling this year. I need you, please, to deliver some gifts for me. Their homes are close by, so it shouldn't take you long by snow machine. I didn't realize they were in need."

"Sure, Mom, I'll do that first thing in the morning tomorrow. I'm happy to do it for you," Andy nodded and smiled. "Too bad you're so banged up, Em, otherwise you could go, too. Have you ever been on a snow machine before?"

"No, but I think I'd like it. Yeah, I can't imagine how fun it would be for me right now." Emily giggled as she held her arms across her ribs. Andy and Betsy both made pained expressions.

"That's really nice, Betsy, that you'd give gifts to those families," Emily said.

"Well, it's the least I can do. We've been so blessed and there's no reason not to share. Even in meager times we should consider others," Betsy said and continued, "There but for the grace of God, go I." She smiled at Emily who contemplated the words.

"And we truly don't know who might be in need, do we?" Emily said, her face studious.

"No, often we don't, except for those who take the time to observe and notice the need. For me, the real joy this time of year is giving. Christmas reflects the good in people that I truly believe exists within us all, except for those whose hearts have hardened and who choose not to be," Betsy said. "And for those souls there is no true happiness, for them everything is not enough. It's unfortunate." Betsy slowly shook her head then smiled.

Andy watched Emily's face as it glowed in the firelight and as she pondered his mother's words. He was captivated not only by her beauty and quick wit but also her keen curiosity and hunger for knowledge. No doubt, he thought, that Emily was a very caring and giving soul. And with Lady having given Em her seal of approval, then that was the final verdict. The two women didn't know why Andy smiled but they returned it just the same.

"Good sermon, Mom," Andy said in jest, as he grinned at Betsy. "And with that ladies, I bid you goodnight. It seems I have more added to my list of things to do tomorrow." He leaned down kissed her forehead.

"Sleep well, Em, I hope you feel much better tomorrow," Andy said, as he smiled down at her and put his hand on her shoulder.

"Thank you, Andy, you as well." Emily looked up and felt the warmth of Andy's smile.

*E*mily had, on her second night, let Lady in her room to sleep. Lady would rest her head on the side of the bed until Emily turned off the lamp. She had grown quite attached to her new companion and the thought of leaving Lady behind saddened her heart. She wondered why her four-legged friend didn't like Cooper, she thought it was strange. But then she remembered that there were no animals at his parents' house and Cooper had never spoken about having had any pets. There was, however, a large stable at Hamilton House filled with beautiful thoroughbreds. But when Emily and Cooper walked out to see them, he spoke of them more as his father's assets, not as animals. As she patted them, he did not. He only spoke of their lineages and chances of ever producing a Triple Crown winner. Emily had been awestruck by the magnificence of the stable, or more correctly, horse mansion. The stable was only a fraction less opulent than Hamilton House and it was a declaration of his parents' wealth. The value of the stable would have housed and fed hundreds of people and educated untold numbers of children. But it was neither her money nor her decisions how it should be spent. Emily sighed and decided it was time for her body and mind to rest.

20

*C*ooper came downstairs early for coffee and to tell Betsy he would skip breakfast, as he had a conference call soon. She gave him a couple biscuits, jam and a bowl of fruit to tide him over.

"Thank you, Betsy, your hospitality is first rate, I commend your efforts. You know, I could arrange for you to have several bed and breakfasts if you'd prefer." Cooper gave her a genuine smile.

"Your offer sounds very generous, but I'm happy here. Thanks, Coop." Betsy returned his smile. "Maybe if I was twenty years younger," she chuckled. "But, no, I like to give my personal touch to each guest."

Cooper nodded and hurried up the stairs with his continental breakfast.

Emily and Andy appeared in the kitchen at the same time. They smiled at each other and Andy pulled a chair out from the table. "For you, madam," he said with a grin.

"Thank you, Andy. You're a gentleman at heart, are you not?" Emily teased.

"For you, of course." He bowed and said, "Coffee or tea, m'lady?"

Emily giggled with less pain than the day before. "Coffee, please."

Betsy turned and chuckled at their exchange. "Good morning you two, help yourselves. I'm almost finished with the waffles and eggs. Hope that meets with your approval, Em."

"My favorite, Betsy. Actually, all the food here is my favorite." Emily giggled and looked at Andy.

Andy set her coffee cup in front of her. "Here you go, Miss Em. Now I need to set the table and help the morning chef, aka, my mom." He smiled and turned to grab the dishes.

"Andy, I'm going to be in the house almost all day with laundry and paperwork. If you don't mind, would you please take care of the barn chores. And you'll also need to do the milking. I'm sure the girls are wondering what happened to us," Betsy said and laughed.

"Sure, Mom, I'd be happy to. The only thing on my list today is clear the driveway again and return a call to Sheriff Ben. He said it wasn't an emergency, so no rush."

"How are you feeling this morning, Em?" Betsy asked.

"I noticed when I laughed earlier it wasn't as painful as yesterday. So, I'd say I'm better." Emily smiled and took a big bite of waffle and rolled her eyes in delight.

Betsy and Andy laughed at her antics. "If you think you're well enough, maybe you'd like to visit our barn family with Andy. He can make sure you don't fall, and I have lots of boots and warm gear for you to wear."

Andy looked at Emily, gave her a broad smile and waited anxiously for her answer. She pointed to her full mouth and chewed as quickly as she could. Betsy laughed.

Emily finally swallowed the last of her bite. "Yes, I'd love to meet them, I hoped I'd be able to before I left. I'm especially excited to meet Max," she said and smiled.

They ate and talked and laughed throughout the rest of their breakfast.

"I'll clean up the kitchen, Andy, if you'll get to the barn, please. And show Emily the closet where she can find the boots, coats and things."

"Will do, Mom. Come on, Em, I hear the cow calling." Andy grinned, and Emily giggled.

"Thanks, Betsy, for another amazing meal. I'll see you a little later," Emily said.

"Okay, you two have fun out there with all the barnyard beasts."

*A*ndy steadied Emily by the arm and a hand on her back. He had cleared the path earlier so there wasn't much snow for her to walk through. "We're not racing, Em. Take your time, I don't want you to fall."

"Me either," she said, and looked up to smile. As they neared the barn, she saw a large, wooden sign above the doors.

Emily laughed. "Noah's Ark, huh? That's hilarious."

They walked into the barn and Andy grabbed a broom to sweep the snow off of Emily's boots. "That's what my dad named this menagerie. My mom decided her guests would enjoy spending time on a real farm. She'd grown a huge garden every year. But to complete their experience, every now and then a truck would show up with animals. And, always, it was two, except the cow. One day my dad watched a truck drive up and unload two goats. That's when he said it was like Noah's Ark. My mom went to town one day and he put the sign up while she was gone. The next morning, he heard her laugh so loud when she saw it. And, well, the two bunnies—she's given away dozens of them." Andy laughed and you could see the love on his face. "Yeah, Dad was always making her laugh."

Emily giggled and said, "I wish I could have met your

father; he had a lot in common with mine, I think. He loved to tease my mom and make her laugh, too."

Andy led Emily to Max's stall. "Emily, meet Max. Max, meet Emily. Now give him the apple," Andy said.

Emily held out her palm with the apple on it. Max gave a little snort and carefully took the treat. "Good boy, Max," Emily said. Max stood close enough for her to stroke his neck. "He's so gentle. Is he that way when you ride him, too?"

"Even better," Andy said. "My dad treated him like his child and Max responded to the love. I think Max still misses Dad. Sometimes when he hears Mom walking toward the barn his ears perk up and he paws the ground and whinnies. But when she walks in, he stops and walks to the back of his stall. We all miss that man; he was a great one." Andy smiled. "Okay, I'm going to delegate. Are you ready, sailor?"

Emily giggled and saluted. "Aye, aye, Cap'n."

Andy completed the barn chores with Emily helping by feeding the chickens. He showed her how to collect the eggs and she was thrilled with each egg she found. Andy laughed at her contagious enthusiasm.

When they left the barn, Emily slipped on some ice under the snow. Before she could hit the ground, Andy caught her in his arms. As he held her, their eyes locked for several seconds. Andy looked worried then and smiled. "Are you okay?" he said.

Emily blushed and smiled. "Yes, but I might be better if I stood up." She giggled.

"Oh, of course," Andy said. His cheeks got redder than from just the cold. He lifted her up and they walked to the house in silence. Each wore a smile.

❄

*B*etsy took the dried towels from the dryer and folded them. As she walked up the stairs, she heard Cooper's voice but not his words. She opened the closet door by his room and clearly heard his conversation.

"Mother, I understand your concern, but it'll work out okay. I know she loves me, and I love her enough," Cooper said. "I know she doesn't come from a money family or a lineage you approve of but she's what I need. That's what appealed to me, her innocence and the fact she hasn't been corrupted by family riches."

Cooper walked to his bedroom window and watched Emily and Andy as they left the barn. He squinted his eyes and his brows furrowed.

"It's not a ploy by her, Mother, she has no ulterior motive. In fact, she didn't know I was rich for six months. That's the reason I bought a cheap little car; I used that to pick her up for our dates. I hated that car, but I needed the assurance she would love me without money. Yes, I know, Father has a prenup drawn up."

Cooper wanted to hang up, but his mother needed to be appeased. His father told him she was still concerned the marriage was wrong. But his nerves were frazzled.

"Look, besides being beautiful, Emily is very intelligent. She'll be quite teachable and I'm sure she won't embarrass you." Cooper snorted. "Well, maybe we need some common blood in our family. I'm sure she feels like Cinderella. Yes, yes, I bought the ring you ordered. I have it with me and I'll propose on New Year's Eve at the party like you planned. Yes, she'll love the ring. What woman would refuse a five carat, emerald-cut diamond engagement ring? She'll be the envy of every woman who sees it. Besides, it'll show off my financial success, right? Of course, there was no problem with her family's background check, I'd already known that. Calm down, Mother. Father wants me married by June. That's part of his master plan. I know if Emily were to have a baby that would keep her busy and fulfilled. But if I'm not happy with Emily in a few years, I'll divorce her. It doesn't have to be forever; it just has to be now. It's that simple. So that'll give you six months to prepare wedding arrangements. I know you can do it, too. I need to go, Mother. I'll see you in a couple days, I hope. Yes, Emily should be fine by then. Talk to you later. Bye.

Betsy stood frozen by what she heard. The magnitude of the implications was damning. She heard Cooper's voice again on another call. She closed the closet door and went downstairs. Betsy put some water on for tea, her face serious and eyes tear-filled. She poured the hot water in the cup and sat down. She started to cry as she stared blankly at the wall. Moments later she heard the front door open and close, as she wiped her face and smiled when Emily and Andy entered the kitchen.

"How 'bout some tea you two?" she said to the rosy-cheeked duo.

$\mathcal{A}$ ndy went into the library and closed the doors behind him. He glanced out of the windows. "I'll never get tired of that," Andy said out loud, to himself, as he gazed at the snowy meadow. He wondered what the sheriff wanted to talk about.

"Hey, Andy, thanks for calling me back. How's everything at Betsy's B&B today?"

"Good morning, Sheriff Ben, all is well up here. Mom said to tell you hi and that she misses you. So, what's going on?" Andy said.

"Well, I won't beat around the bush. I'd like for you to be my deputy. You're the most honorable man I've known, after your dad of course. I want to retire in a couple of years, and you'd step right into my position. That would give time for all the county and state officials to come to know and respect you, too. I spoke with the mayor and town attorney, they're in agreement. This town loves you, Andy, and you always help before you're even asked. I know you have a heart for this town and its people. We would all be proud to have you as our sheriff one day. Think about it and give me your answer after the first of the year. That's about the time I'd want you to start. Parsons needs you, Andy."

"I'm kind of speechless right now, Ben. I never imagined anything like this before. I appreciate your offer and vote of confidence. But you know, I promised Mom that I would never again have a job that required me to carry a gun. So, it's really her decision. Let me discuss it with her. She's a tough lady, but I wouldn't want this to put an unwanted burden on her. She's already spent a lot of years worried I wasn't coming home. I'm mighty proud that you have asked me, however the outcome goes. You've been my second father and I respect what you do. I'll let you know as soon as I have a private moment with Mom."

"I want what's best for Betsy, too. She deserves to reap all the happiness she's sown over the years, her entire life in fact. I'll absolutely stand by whatever decision you make. Give your mom a kiss for me, okay? Take care. Bye."

"I will and you take care, too. Bye." Andy put his phone down and stared out the window.

21

*E*mily was reading some framed letters and looking at a wall of family photographs by the library doors. Andy opened the doors and they were both surprised at how near they were to each other. Emily caught a whiff of peppermint again.

"Oh, hi, Andy," Emily said. "I was looking at all these pictures. And the framed letters. These are wonderful."

"Hi, Em," Andy said with a huge grin on his face. "Yeah, I look at all those pretty often, too. It reminds me how important family is and the history and memories that go along with those faces. I was just coming out to get you. If we hurry, you'll be able to see deer out in the meadow; they're feeding on some bushes."

Andy grabbed Emily's hand and pulled her firmly but not so fast as to hurt her. Lady didn't let much space get between her and Emily. They stopped in front of the library windows with Lady within reach and she sat at Emily's feet watching her every move.

Emily gasped as she stepped closer to the glass. Her face lit up with the biggest smile Andy had seen on her. Her eyes were wide in wonder as she watched the deer move slowly about the meadow, unaware of their audience. She grew still and he saw the amazement on her face as a tear crept down her cheek. In her eyes he saw the reflection of the beauty and majesty as she saw it. Andy felt the defenses which surrounded his heart slip away; he knew he was entirely and wholly at her mercy. He tucked this moment into the forever part of his memories. She would be gone even before the embers in the fireplace had cooled and this would be all he had left of her. This brief interval would need to last a lifetime —and longer.

"Thank you," Emily said and looked up at Andy with a contented smile, then turned and walked toward his desk to look at his medals. She stopped in front of the framed awards and commendations.

"You're a brave man, Andy. I've never known a hero before, someone with so much courage. I guess I'd considered my parents as my heroes." Her smile faded as she looked away to hide her tears. "They were killed in a plane accident, though, and that's why I'm afraid to fly. But that led me here in a car crash and I met you." She looked up and into Andy's eyes with a soft smile.

"I was afraid all the time in Afghanistan," Andy said. "So many men depended on me to keep them alive. And I promised them all I would never ask them to do anything that I wouldn't. Each of my guys deserved those medals. As far as brave, you just need to have enough courage for one more minute, one minute at a time." Andy had never shared that with anyone before, but he trusted Emily and her friendly smile.

"Thank you for those words; it gives me a different perspective. If you could face such danger, then I suppose getting on an airplane would not be impossible for me to do —one minute and one step at a time."

They turned to leave when Emily noticed a chess board she hadn't seen in the corner.

"Do you play chess, Andy?" Emily looked intrigued.

"I used to play with my dad, he taught me, but I haven't touched it since he died. I don't know anyone that plays."

"Well, if you're lucky I might let you lose," Emily giggled. "It was my dad, too, that showed me how to play. It took me seven years to finally beat him and he was so proud that we went out for pizza and ice cream and he asked everyone there to applaud my achievement. I was so embarrassed that I would've crawled under the table, but my mom stopped me. I've always been a bit shy and that nearly painted a permanent red on my face. I've asked a couple of people I know, too, but also never found anyone interested in playing."

"I hope we have a chance to play," Andy said with a smirk, "to see who had the better teacher."

They laughed and promised to revisit the challenge they'd made.

Cooper came down early for dinner but seemed distracted, as if something weighed heavily on his mind. He looked at Betsy and his demeanor changed.

"Good evening, Betsy, dinner smells good as always." He poured some iced tea and sat near the counter.

"Hello, Cooper," Betsy returned the pleasantry. "I trust you've conquered the world today," Betsy said with a smile, but her face registered some concern or worry.

Cooper smiled back. "Yes, as a matter of fact. I think I have a good handle on all that should be accomplished by the end of the month and into the new year. With the exception, of course, not being at the right place. But that should change soon. Have you heard any news about the snow?"

"I spoke with Sheriff Ben earlier, he said we may have a slight break tomorrow and for a couple of days, according to information he received. Hopefully, they can get the roads cleared before Christmas so you can be with your parents."

"Good, that sounds promising. I'll call my father with the news. He's planned to send a car for us as soon as the weather permitted. It's about a four-hour drive from here to Hamilton House."

"Andy has kept our driveway cleared enough to connect to the main road. But the road crew hasn't been able to make it out this far yet. The sheriff promised he'd get the snow plows out this far as soon as possible, while there's a break in the snowfall. Another storm is brewing and expected to bring more snow on Christmas night. However, Mother Nature may have other plans."

Cooper nodded. "Yes, some things are not always predictable as much as we'd like them to be, are they?" Cooper's words seemed to mean more than just the weather. "So, Betsy, what else have you done in your life besides this B&B? Have you always lived here?"

"Yes, my family has lived in Parsons for generations. My great-grandparents settled here long ago. The story is they arrived here in the spring, when the iris was in bloom. My grandmother was so captivated by the beautiful flowers that covered the base of the mountain. She refused to live anywhere else and lovingly referred to her new home as Iris Peak. They were among the first to settle here. Local folks adopted the name until years later when the people began to call this Glimmer Mountain," Betsy said as she continued to cook dinner.

Cooper nodded his head slightly. "That's an interesting story."

"I know what your father does, but tell me, what does your mother do with her time?" Betsy asked.

Cooper chuckled. "She spends money, travels with friends and hosts social gatherings. Her life is full, and she seems content to busy herself while my father builds his empire." Cooper laughed. His phone rang and he excused himself.

Betsy was saddened by the answer Cooper had given about his mother. It explained, however, a lot about the man she'd just spoken with.

Andy and Emily walked into the kitchen as they laughed. "Hi, Mom."

"Betsy, I just saw the most enchanting scene from the library windows," Emily gushed. I'll never forget watching the deer in the meadow, I'll treasure that memory forever. It was breathtaking."

"And I enjoyed watching Em's face," Andy added as they smiled at each other.

"That's wonderful," Betsy said. "I never tire of looking out there. I always see something different and beautiful. As the seasons change, I remember moments that have happened in my life, standing in front of those very windows. It's a way to not let life just pass without thought. Time seems to move more slowly here, I think. Or, perhaps, this house and that view make you more mindful of even the smallest changes and movements."

"Wow, Mom, that's pretty profound for so late in the day," Andy teased with a huge grin.

Betsy laughed, and raised the spoon she held as if to smack him. "Once a teacher, always a teacher," Betsy said with a loving smile.

Emily giggled. "Watch out for the cook armed with a spoon."

They all laughed at the kitchen antics. Betsy was happy for their company; it distracted her thoughts from what she'd heard earlier that day.

Cooper returned and joined them for dinner. As the food was passed, Emily recounted the wall of family photos she'd seen earlier.

"I saw a photo of you, I think, standing with a woman who looked very much like you, but in younger days. Is that your sister, Estelle?" Emily asked.

"Much younger days," Betsy chuckled. "Yes, that's my sister and my accomplice."

"I stared at that photo for a long time and thought how confusing it must have been to tell which face belonged to which name," Emily said and laughed.

"That's right, dear, and we liked to keep them guessing," Betsy said, and giggled.

"From the moment I saw you on the porch, I kept thinking you looked so familiar. But I couldn't quite understand why. I considered that the reason could be I'd just suffered a concussion." Emily smiled but Cooper frowned at his plate. "I was glad when Andy told me you had a twin sister at the antique store. I've had a feeling of deja vu since I've been here. You both exhibit the same kindness in what you do and the way you show it, and it's written on your faces. There—that's my essay on twins. Now I can eat this magnificent dinner." Emily giggled and raised a forkful of food. "Here's to twins and the cook." Everyone, except Cooper, raised their forks to the toast.

"Dessert tonight is something special, one of my favorites," Betsy said with a childish look on her face. "Tonight, it's marshmallows at the fireplace." She grinned and pulled a big bag of the white, fluffy delights out of the cabinet. "And I have the ingredients to make s'mores, too." Her smile reflected her joy in roasting marshmallows. They all laughed.

Emily knew Cooper would go upstairs and that suited her fine. She had come to love the time spent in the evenings at the fireplace with Betsy and Andy. She had quickly become quite attached to this family and the surroundings. Although she had to suffer some pain on the road to this place, she was more than happy to have paid the price to be with them.

hen Emily and Lady entered the kitchen, Cooper had just sat down at the table.

"Good morning, Emily. How are you feeling today?" Cooper said to her. He was careful not to encroach on Lady's space under the table.

As she reached for her chair, Andy stood and pulled it out for her. "Thank you, Andy. It's still a bit difficult to manage these heavy chairs," Emily said and smiled at Andy. She looked at Cooper and said, "Better, but I still have limitations and these chairs are one of them." Cooper had a sheepish look on his face that didn't last long. He glared at Andy, but it went unnoticed.

"Well, all those bruised muscles and soft tissue will take a while longer to heal. But I think you've come a long way from the first night here," Betsy said. "And I prescribe more time resting in front of the fireplace." She smiled at Emily.

"Those naps on the couch are the best ever, and it doesn't take long for the fire to put me to sleep after one of these meals," Emily giggled. "It's probably better than a sleeping pill. It's so relaxing."

"I made an extra pan of the blueberry muffins. They're

great for a mid-day snack with your tea," Betsy said, as she smiled and took a bite of her muffin.

When breakfast was finished, Betsy went to the barn to take care of her animals. Cooper had gone upstairs to wait for a call. Emily helped Andy with the dishes and cleanup.

As she handed him more plates she smiled, and said, "I've noticed that you like peppermint candies—a lot." She giggled and met his eyes. "Care to elaborate on your addiction?"

Andy laughed. "Oh, you noticed, did you?" He looked down as he continued to wash a plate. "Well, short story, it reminds me of my dad." Andy stopped and looked at Emily with a serene look on his face. "He loved the peppermints that mom only set out at Christmas time. He asked her several years ago if he could have them all year long. Mom said she was really surprised by his request but assured him he could. Almost daily, at some point in time, you would find him with a mint in his mouth, accompanied by a happy mood. It seemed more than just a penchant for the flavor. Curiosity got the better of my mom and she finally asked him why he suddenly wanted more mints. This was my dad's response:

'Well, Betsy, these remind me of Christmas, and you know how much I love that time of year. People are kinder and more giving. I wish it could be Christmas all year. When I put one of these candies in my mouth—it reminds me of all the good feelings. And it reminds me to be a better person.'

So, every now and then, I pop a peppermint, think of him —and try to be like my father."

Emily had stopped moving as she listened. "Your dad was a very wise man," she said and smiled.

❄

*a*ndy had just walked Emily in to sit by the fire when his phone rang.

"Hey, Sheriff, what's up?" Andy said in a cheery voice.

"We have a situation, Andy. The Sanders boys decided early this morning to deliver Christmas gifts to their grandparents. Since the snow slowed down, they wanted to visit grandma and grandpa. They took their phone and were instructed to call as soon as they got there. Unfortunately, the boys took both snow machines, which Matt said not to do. One of the machines has a mechanical issue. The boys were gone before he could stop them. Matt said he doesn't have another machine to look for them himself. That was about 90 minutes ago, and it only takes thirty minutes to get to his parents' house. He's called his folks, but they haven't seen the boys. Matt's called his son's phone several times but there's no answer. I don't want to wait any longer to start a search, it gets dark pretty early now. Can you meet me and the other boys at marker seventy-two in about thirty minutes?"

"Sure. I'll see you there. Bye." Andy rushed to tell Betsy about the emergency. They packed and gathered all the essentials as they had many times before.

"Be safe, Andy," Betsy said as she hugged him. "Wait, wear this, too. I'll be there with you," Betsy said as she wrapped a bright, neon-green scarf around his neck and tucked it into his jacket. Emily watched and felt worried. It seemed that this time it was different.

"I'll see you at dinner time, Andy," Emily said and put on a brave smile.

Andy smiled back and nodded. "I'll come home, I promise," he said. He waved to the women then pushed his machine at full throttle down the driveway.

Betsy saw the distress on Emily's face. "He'll be okay, Em. And we'll be telling stories and eating peach cobbler by the fire tonight." Betsy, too, wore a brave face as she smiled and said a silent prayer for her son's safe return. She told herself it would be alright as they walked back into the house.

*C*ooper went upstairs and saw he missed a call—it was Charlotte. He was expecting a call from one of his clients instead. He wished his mother had gotten over Charlotte as he had done. It distressed him when plans went sideways, and he did his best not to let that happen. He found it easier when it came to business, but it was more difficult with personal matters. He had wondered about Charlotte several times since they'd spoken. He tried to purge his thoughts, but it was a distraction hard to erase. His mother's interference had caused the mess. Now what he needed to do was ignore Charlotte and tell his mother to uninvite her from all future social functions where he would be included. Emily was the plan now, not Charlotte. His phone rang again, and it was the business call he expected.

*T*he women sat by the fireplace in silence as they stared at the flames. Betsy stood and stretched.

"Well, I have calls to return and to follow up on some folks. Would you like another cup of tea, dear?"

"No, thank you, Betsy. I need to get up and move around. I think I'll see what movie is playing on the window in the library," Emily said, as she giggled.

Betsy grinned. "I like your sense of humor. Okay, then, remember to just forage in the kitchen if you get hungry." Betsy turned and left the room.

Emily walked to the library doors and stopped. There were still some framed messages on the walls she hadn't read. The first one she saw was cross stitched.

"But the greatest of these is love."

She remembered the passage but couldn't remember where it was in the Bible. She would have to look that up. She wondered who had done the sewing, she'd ask Betsy. Next was a handwritten note. The paper was yellowed but the penmanship was excellent, from a bygone era before electronics had stolen the art of cursive.

"I will never break your heart, Elizabeth Parsons.

I will protect it as my own. I love you. —Hank"

Emily read those words and imagined how great their love had been. From what she was told, piecing together moments from their lives as husband and wife, Hank and Betsy's had been a grand love story. She hoped someday to feel that connected, to be so linked in mind and spirit with the one you loved, that even in death their presence was still felt.

*E*mily sighed and walked into the library and stood before the view of the snowy world outside. Today there were no deer. But she still felt the same sense of wonder and she knew that no matter what, the deer would come again. She heard footsteps and turned to see Cooper approach.

"Hi, Cooper, it's good to see you, you're down early. Is work all finished for today?" Emily said, as she reached out to hug him. He stopped just short of her and seemed perturbed.

"Did you have fun in the barn yesterday with Andy?" Cooper said. Before Emily could answer he continued. "I saw from my window that you almost fell. Lucky he was there to catch you. I must say, Emily, you seem rather taken with him. A silly crush, perhaps?"

"I went out to see the farm animals, that's all. I needed to go outside for a bit, and he was kind enough to help me," Emily said. "Which is more than I can say for you. You've barely spoken to me since we've been here. And left me to be cared for by strangers, nice strangers, but strangers none the less. Not once have you brought me a cup of tea or offered to rub my stiff neck. Which by the way, you caused. Do you even care?" Emily released the emotional hurt that had built up.

Cooper chose not to answer, he'd achieved what he wanted. He had let Emily know he was aware of her attraction to Andy, but since it would only be short term he chose not to argue. Instead, he wandered toward the desk and saw Andy's medals and letters of commendation. And several photos of him in uniform. He looked formidable.

"Well, it seems that our humble country boy is a war hero. He's never mentioned it."

"Real heroes don't brag, Coop," Emily said intentionally and with contempt in her voice.

Cooper let her attitude and words slide off. "Well, if he were to talk about those medals, he could monetize his position, financially or politically—even both. But some people settle for unremarkable lives. Oh well, his loss," Cooper said nonchalantly. He turned and walked away; he appeared to be happy with how he'd handled her.

Emily seethed. Cooper had no right to be so disrespectful to her or to Andy. She turned and stood in front of the windows again. Even the glass panorama didn't improve her disposition. She refocused her eyes and saw the reflection of an unhappy woman.

*B*etsy returned to see Emily sitting by the fire with a cup of tea. She set a small plate of cookies on the side table, stoked the logs and turned to Emily. "Are you alright, dear?"

Emily sighed and said, "Not really, Cooper and I had words—not very nice words."

"It would be hard not to do under the circumstances. Is there anything I can do for you?"

"Just sit with me, please. You have a calming effect." Emily smiled at Betsy.

"Of course, that's what I'd planned, complete with Christmas cookies. Those always make me feel better." The women giggled. Emily exhaled and, in fact, felt better.

23

*A*ndy saw the group of men ahead and powered toward them. When he reached them, he pulled up beside Ben and turned off his snow machine. "Hi, Sheriff. What's the plan?"

"It's been two hours now and still no word from the boys. Their dad told me what their usual route was, but if the boys got off the trail it could mean a lot more territory to cover. We're looking for a bright yellow jacket and bright blue jacket, black helmets and one white machine and one black. Got it? Everyone has their phones and flares, right?" Sheriff Ben looked around the circle of men. "And avalanche trans-ceivers, binoculars and shovels? Make sure your flags are secured so we can see each other." The party all shook their heads and reached back to feel their antenna flags. "Good. Okay, I want half of us to go directly to Matt's. I want you to lead that, Andy. And the other half go with me, to the grand-parents' house, George and Gracie's place. We'll meet in the middle but try to fan out as best you can. Go slow, there's a lot of downed trees from last year's fire up there. Be sure to check the river in case they tried to cross; it's not totally frozen yet. And we're quite a way below the road here, so watch for any slides that may have happened. Keep your eyes open men. We only have a few hours of daylight left to find them. Watch out for each other and be safe out there." The men automatically fell in behind the sheriff and Andy as they left their meeting area. Time was running out. It would be a very cold night to be outside.

The machines roared off, as red flags waved, in a flurry of snow that slowly drifted back to the frozen ground. The sound of the search party came from two distinct locations and distances. Gradually the sound of the engines faded into the wintry woods.

The father of the missing boys came out of his house when he heard the snow machines approach. Worry was written on his face. Anxiety and tension had knotted every muscle in his body and guilt weighed him down. He looked much smaller than he really was. He should have taken the time to watch the boys before they left, gave them warnings about the trail and explained again the necessity of taking only one snowmobile. Matt was stranded the day before by the faulty machine. It had worked fine, until it didn't. He managed to bring it back to life and drive it home. If anything happened to those boys, his sense of failure and loss would haunt him until his last breath. He tried to release all that with a smile as Andy drove up.

"Hey, Andy. Boys," Matt said, as he glanced at each one. "Thanks for being here."

"Hi, Matt. Don't worry, we're gonna bring your boys back to you today. Tell me again, how they usually go to your folks' house?"

"In the winter we follow the trail beside the river. But with those heavy rains this year, the river flooded its banks in several places. So, there's no established trail like before and this heavy snowfall will have covered my tracks from my visit over there a few days ago. I shouldn't have let them go, but they were excited the snow stopped because they wanted to deliver their gifts to their grandparents before the next storm."

"Don't blame yourself, Matt. They're teenagers now, so you expect they can be more independent. We'll find them for you. The sheriff and his guys should be at your parents' house now. The plan is for us to meet up at the midpoint on the trail. I know these woods really well so we're gonna find them, maybe a bit cold but otherwise okay."

"Thanks, Andy. Oh, I forgot to tell you that there are emergency flares in the storage under each seat on the machines." Matt's face had grown haggard and his jaws were clenched.

"That's good to know," Andy said. "Okay, let's get moving. Bye, Matt."

Matt stood and watched as the search party veered toward the river. He said a silent prayer for the safe return of his sons.

Sheriff Ben had met with the grandparents and was on the trail by the river. There had been a lot of trails from the cross-country skiers but those were now covered in a thick layer of snow. The men fanned out across the area where they guessed the two boys might have gone. Andy's team worked the other end from Matt's house in the same fashion. It was slow but the men took their time and looked for any and all details. Several times Ben and Andy stopped to use their binoculars in hopes of spotting something, anything to give a clue of the boys' whereabouts. Andy's group was able to find tracks that weaved in between the trees, sometimes close to the river, other times quite a distance away from it. It appeared the boys were creating their own way to George and Gracie's house. Often times, the tracks would split up, not following each other. Other times, the tracks were too close to the riverbank, which was hard to see, hidden beneath the snow, brush and fallen trees. The young spruce hid the water's edge below. The terrain was filled with thickets of tall pine and many rock outcroppings. It was difficult to clearly see.

After about five miles Andy spotted some black oil on the snow. He expected to find the faulty machine up a little way, and he hoped the boys would be there, too. As he and his men rounded a large rock formation, they found the broken snow machine abandoned. Andy stopped to speak to the sheriff.

"Hey, Ben, we found one of the machines, the black one, it's abandoned. Both boys are headed in your direction on one machine, the white one. I don't see a lot of footprints, so they didn't spend much time here."

"Okay, good to know, Andy. We'll look for the boys on a white machine then. Thanks," Sheriff Ben said.

*T*anner and Scott didn't think about how little of the trail they would be able to see. But with all this new snow off-trail driving should be okay. They took it much slower than usual but still it was fun in the deep snow. After an hour or so Scott's snowmobile started cutting out. Finally, the engine stalled, it died and couldn't be restarted. Scott hopped on with his brother, Tanner, and didn't notice that his phoned dropped out of his unzipped pocket. They continued their Christmas gifts delivery to their grandparents, the brown duffel bag on Scott's lap.

The machine sat lower in the snow with the two boys riding it. Tanner had been able to glide over the top of most of the rough terrain but with the extra weight it had become a problem. He didn't want to bottom out on any rocks or trees, so he moved closer to the river, where he felt sure to catch a smoother ride. During the unusually heavy summer rains parts of the river flooded, and the banks were pushed wider than before. It was impossible to see some areas of ice-covered water due to the bushes and small trees. As Tanner rounded a patch of short willows the tips of his skis fell downward over a four-foot embankment under the snow, and the machine dropped down, skidded for several feet then broke through the ice and into five feet of freezing water. Tanner was thrown over the windshield as Scott jumped toward the bushes and managed to pull himself up on the bank. Tanner struggled to free himself of the ice and to position himself toward his brother. He was partially submerged as was his machine.

"Tanner. Tanner," Scott yelled. He pushed down a tall tree sapling toward his brother. "Here, grab this limb and pull yourself up."

Tanner's arms and legs were heavy with river water soaked into his outer garments and his muscles were cold and refused to move as rapidly as he commanded. In a matter of minutes, Scott was able to grab his brother's hand and wrist to pull him up out of the icy water. Fortunately for the boys the temperature wasn't sub-zero, but it was cold enough for a drenched body to suffer hypothermia in a matter of minutes. Only Scott's legs below his knees had fallen into the water. He knew he needed to warm Tanner's body. He'd worn several layers of clothing to keep warm that day while out riding. Already Tanner was shivering uncontrollably, and his arms and legs felt numb.

"Okay, Tanner, we need to get your wet clothes off. You can wear my jacket and snow pants. I have extra gloves in the pockets, too," Scott said, as he worked to undress himself.

"Alright, thanks. I'm sorry I just didn't see it. Are you okay?" Tanner said. He wasn't able to control his body. He tried to take his jacket off, but his fingers and hands were numb and clumsy.

"I got it, Tanner. Yeah, I'm good," Scott said, as he quickly removed his brother's jacket and shirts and covered him with his own jacket. Tanner moaned as he tried to stand.

"I think I messed up my knee, I can't put any weight on it," Tanner said.

"Okay, just hold on to me," Scott said, as he peeled off the rest of the wet clothes and helped Tanner into the dry ones. As his brother warmed up, Scott reached into his pocket for the phone. When he felt the pocket open, he had a sick feeling in his stomach. The phone was missing. He began to feel cold, but he knew they were only a few miles away from a warm house. He looked at the partially submerged machine and remembered there were flares under the seat, but he couldn't risk falling in the water. There was no more extra, dry clothing and as it was, he began to shiver. It would be a slow walk with Tanner's injured knee, but he hoped they could make it before dark. The wind had begun to blow with an occasional gust and the sky had filled with thick, ominous clouds. At this higher elevation extreme winter weather happened often and with little warning.

24

*S*heriff Murphy made visual on the boys with his binoculars. They were on foot and one seemed to be injured and carried a duffel bag. Ben noticed there was only a bright blue jacket being worn.

Andy had just stopped and turned off his engine to check for messages when the sheriff's call came through.

"Hey, Ben, I'm hoping you have good news for me. Come on, make this a good day," Andy said, as he kept an eye on his team as they slowly searched the wooded area.

"Yep, I just put eyes on the boys. They're on foot and looks like one may have a leg injury. We should be with them shortly. You and your team are probably closer to this end now so just meet us at George and Gracie's house. Be careful. See you soon."

"That's great news. We'll be there ASAP then. Bye." Andy's team had noticed he stopped, so one by one they had let the other team members know. Andy waved them in and told them the boys were found and they could follow him to the grandparents' house.

It took about twenty minutes to get to the boys. The men put a warm jacket on Scott and both boys were wrapped in blankets. Scott and Tanner took turns as they explained what happened. Hand warmers were put in the boys' jacket pockets and then they mounted the machines of their rescuers.

"Oh, no—wait," Scott shouted, as he held out his hand. "I dropped my phone back there; it must be by the other snow machine. I unzipped my pocket for something when I got on with Tanner. My dad will kill me." Scott shook his head as he lowered it.

"That's okay, boy, calm down," Ben said, as he smiled. "I'll let the other team know and they can locate your phone for you. You already survived near death once today, that's enough." Before the group returned to George and Gracie's house the sheriff called Andy.

"No problem, Sheriff. We're probably getting close to your proximity, so I'll send my team ahead to meet you. I've got a good trail now to follow, so I'll go back for the boy's phone, it can't have gone too far. I knew I should've taken a closer look over there. But I was trying to find boys not phones," Andy said and laughed.

"Okay, thanks, I'll let him know I've got my best man on it. Be safe, Andy, it looks like the weather may be turning on us," Ben said and looked at the foreboding sky.

"Always. Besides, I promised someone I'd be home for dinner. You know a little snow won't stop me. Bye." Andy smiled as he thought about Emily and how easy it was to make her laugh.

*A*ndy looked up at the darkening sky and ominous clouds and decided he shouldn't waste any time finding the phone. The wind picked up which wasn't unusual in this area, being so close to Squall Pass. Winter months often brought hurricane-type winds through the mountains where drifts could easily bury a snowplow. Sheriff Thomas, in Oakville, had already closed the road on the other side of the pass in late November, until early spring after the roads were clear of any ice. Squall Pass was so dangerous it was decided years ago to reroute traffic to a new highway. These days the old mountain road was mostly for tourists during the summer months who desired to see the stunning scenery and take pictures for their scrapbooks back home.

As Andy gunned his throttle, he was careful to stay on his earlier path and avoid anything that protruded through the snow and the overhanging tree branches. He knew he'd lose the light soon and, although he had a headlight, it would be difficult. The closer he got to the abandoned machine the more he felt a growing sense of dread. He hadn't spotted the phone on the trail but saw the machine up ahead and felt relieved that he'd soon turn around and head for a warm place by the fire and a hot cup of coffee. Still, he couldn't shake the knot that had grown in his gut; he knew it was much more than the impending darkness. Andy searched the ground beside and all around the broken machine but still didn't find what he was looking for. He stood back and studied the view and there, lying on the black footrest, was the black phone. It wouldn't have been noticed as the boys hurried off.

*A*bove Andy, Squall Pass brewed a threatening mixture of winds and heavy snowfall. A moist, warm air mass rose from below and created a rare instability. The additional upward motion of air increased the snow growth, but more importantly, it caused enough electrical separation within the clouds for lightning to strike. Several strikes above the pass and the reverberation from the deafening thunder began to affect the deep-packed snow on the mountain peaks.

The power and force of the lightning strikes caused a vibration that moved and stressed the snowpack. The last snowfall was still loose and began to slide downhill, gaining momentum exponentially, further and faster. As small cracks formed in the compressed snow it loosened the grip strength of the layer upon layer of ice beneath it. It had been several generations since the snowpack on Glimmer Mountain had moved. But this winter, and this weather, created a monumental shift and an avalanche had begun. The ice slabs broke free and hurtled downward, crashing into the rocks below and spewing large chunks and deadly shards into the air. Large stands of trees were wiped from the face of the mountain. The snow and ice mounted a deadly attack on anything below in their path.

Sheriff Ben and his team of men took some time upon their delivery of the cold and missing grandsons, and warmed up at the grandparents' house. Grandma Gracie determined that Tanner only had a sprained knee and both of her grandsons suffered bruised egos but were otherwise in good shape. Grandpa George took the opportunity to instill more life lessons into their experience. Scott was commended for his quick thinking to save his brother from further hypothermia and possible serious complications. After some coffee and homemade bread and jelly, the team of rescuers walked out to return home. Ben looked up and saw the first bolt of lightning, and they all heard the subsequent thunder boom over the peaks and into the valley below. Time and again the lightning and thunder occurred in quick succession. Ben understood the consequence of what had happened and what would follow. He called Andy, again and again, but no answer. He left a message. "Andy, get out of there now," Ben shouted into his phone. "It's an avalanche." As Ben picked up his binoculars, and as he watched the snow begin to slide down the mountainside, his chest tightened, and he held his breath. With panic in his voice, he released the air in his lungs. "Please, Lord, protect Andy and bring him back home alive." Ben called Matt and told him what he'd seen. As soon as the slide stopped, he would send some of his men back in his direction to find Andy. Ben then called two other men in town with instructions where to meet him and to bring their search dogs.

Ben watched the exact location and progression of the tonnage of snow and ice that barreled down the mountainside. He determined at that weight and size the avalanche would easily cross the highway in an explosion of ice and snow and pour down over the low-lying cliff to the river area below. There would only be a small window of time for Andy to escape the center of the angry devastation. And from Andy's location he wouldn't see the tsunami of snow coming at him until it was almost too late. Ben hoped Andy had a sixth sense and knew how to use it.

*A*s Andy straddled his snow machine, he heard the first boom of thunder. He looked up and saw a bolt of lightning and heard the second deafening sound. That foreboding he felt earlier suddenly rushed back into his consciousness, along with the familiar fight or flight sensation he'd known in Afghanistan. Again, he heard the crack of the thunderclap. Instantly he knew the right and immediate decision—was flight. Andy started his machine, stood up on the runners as he gunned the engine and spun his machine around. He raced toward George and Gracie's house. Several times he almost lost control because of the unpredictable trail. Above the roar of the engine he still heard more thunder and a loud rumbling. He glanced over his shoulder in time to see the eruption of snow and ice as it exploded over the side of the highway above. He knew the avalanche was on a collision course aimed at him. As he rode ahead of the onslaught he gulped as much air as he could to fill his lungs. The torrent of white crashed below, and it blasted and smothered everything in its path. He had little time to plan his escape as the surge of snow caught up to him, hit him from the side and swept him off the snow machine. He struggled to keep his bearings even as he was enveloped by this cold, white adversary. It was a constant crush as he was pushed further and further. He fought to raise his arms out and above his head as he kicked his legs and pulled the snow with his hands. If he had any chance of surviving, he needed to be on or as close to the surface as possible. He was stabbed and beaten by objects in the snow, but he determined he wouldn't quit as long as his body could move. The closer to the edge of the snow mass, the closer he would be to being rescued. His will to live brought him home from war. This was a different enemy but the only way to defeat it was to remain calm and in control of his mind and emotions. Now was not the time to panic, if ever. He felt the pressure against his body lessen and the push slowed down and then he came to a rest. He slowly pulled his hand back to his face and carved out a breathing space in the snow. Next he reached out again in what he believed to be upward toward the sky. His hand wasn't free from the packed snow. The most he could hope for now was to be discovered by a search and rescue team. He felt comforted to know that Sheriff Ben would already have formed one—for him this time. Although he'd worn his transceiver, it was set to receive mode in the event one of the team members was lost earlier. He tried to reach it but something was wedged on top of it. Without a transmitted signal he knew his rescue would be delayed. It was up to him to stay alive until the morning and hope he was close enough to the surface that the dogs could locate him.

25

*A*s Betsy and Emily walked from the kitchen, they heard a distant thunder. They walked to the library window and saw several lightning strikes above the mountains as they admired the meadow view. Betsy commented she had never seen lightning up there before but the weather at Squall Pass was notorious for being unpredictable.

Betsy and Emily had just finished their tea and cookies by the fire when Betsy's phone rang. She glanced down and saw it was the sheriff.

"Hi, Ben, did you find the boys?" Betsy said, in a hopeful tone.

"Yes, we did and they're fine. But there was an avalanche on Squall Pass that crossed the road and spilled into the valley. Andy was by the river and now he's missing."

Betsy gasped. "Oh, no, Ben." Her eyes welled with tears.

Ben continued. "He'd gone back to find one of the boys' phone and I figure he was in the snow's path. The slide was massive and after the snow stopped, we tried to find him, but it got too dark. We checked as much of the perimeter as we could but there was no sign of Andy. I'm sure his beacon was switched to receive rather than transmit in case one of our team had gotten lost during the first search. He wouldn't have expected to be caught in an avalanche. Tomorrow we'll start the search again at daylight. Tonight, I'm calling the governor for assistance. I'll find our boy, Betsy, and you know how strong he is. When we find him, he'll probably ask me what took so long." Sheriff Ben gave a small laugh and tried to lift her spirits as much as he could. "I'm sure I'll bring him home safe and in one piece, Betsy. Love you. Bye."

"Thanks, Ben. Keep me posted, please. Bye." Betsy sat her phone on her lap.

Emily heard Betsy gasp and saw the horrified look on her face. Her heart fell into her stomach. She knew something had happened to Andy. She didn't know what, but it was bad.

"What is it, Betsy? Did Andy get hurt?" Emily said in an anxious voice.

"No. He's missing. Remember the lightning and thunder earlier this afternoon? It caused a massive avalanche. The sheriff thinks Andy is buried somewhere in it or hurt and can't move." Betsy held her head in her hands. Andy had come back from war and now this. She lifted her head again. No, she refused to give up.

"What are they going to do?" Emily said.

"They searched as long as possible before it got dark. They'll start again first thing in the morning. The only thing any of us can do tonight—is pray."

Cooper had come downstairs when Betsy was on the phone. He heard her explain to Emily the details of her conversation with Ben. He observed the reaction on Emily's face before he walked into the living room. He stood near Betsy's chair and looked down at her with concern written on his face.

"Betsy, I'm so sorry to hear about Andy," Cooper said. "If I can help in any way, please, let me know. My father may have resources that can be of use."

"Thank you, Cooper, sincerely." Betsy smiled up at

Cooper. "I think right now I just need another cup of tea. Em, would you like a refill? Care to join us, Coop? I have cookies." Betsy looked at him with a weak smile.

They walked into the kitchen and as Betsy put their steaming cups of tea down on the table, Lady walked from Emily to Betsy and laid her head on her knee.

Betsy reached down and stroked Lady on the head. "Thanks, Lady. You know, don't you girl? He'll be okay—I'm sure," Betsy said to the dog and herself.

Cooper chose to finish his tea and cookies upstairs as he waited for another call.

Betsy and Emily sat in silence and sipped their cups of calm. Betsy continued to stroke Lady then she looked at Emily and smiled.

"It's Glimmer Mountain, Em—remember?" Emily returned Betsy's weak smile.

$\mathcal{B}$en decided to call the governor and not wait until morning. They had been friends since their teams had competed in high school athletics. They'd kept in touch through the years and through the political campaigns. Ben needed help so he called in a favor.

"Hello, Governor. This is Sheriff Murphy calling," Ben said.

"Hey, Ben, you old dog. What's got you calling me at night and not during office hours. An emergency?" Governor Harris asked.

"Yeah, Pete, you may not have heard yet, but we just had a massive avalanche up Squall Pass way. I had a search today for two lost teenagers, who we found in good condition. But I think my deputy got caught in it and is buried somewhere. We were only able to search for him a short time before it got too dark. It would help if we could get the road cleared up that way from Parsons," Ben said.

"That is a big emergency, Ben. I can send the plows up tonight to be in place for in the morning," Governor Harris said. "Say, Ben, I didn't know you had a deputy. What's his name?"

"It's not official yet, but it's Andy Walker. I just asked him a couple days ago. I told him to take a few days to think about it. He didn't even get that chance."

"The war hero?" Governor Harris' voice sounded incredulous. "There's no way we can't find him, Ben. We need every hero we can get. What else do you need?"

"Well, the slide was so big I don't think any more snow would move if we had a helicopter up there to get a bird's eye view. That could help us find him faster, don't ya think?" Ben said.

"That's a good idea. Send me the coordinates of an approximation of his whereabouts and I'll pass that along and have a bird in the sky at daybreak. Good luck finding your deputy, Ben. I know he's a fine man, I'm familiar with his story. And I remember his mom, too. You were pretty sweet on her, weren't you, but who could resist Hank?" the governor chuckled. "Call me tomorrow with any news and I'll say a prayer to the big guy. Goodbye, my friend."

"Thanks, Pete, much appreciated. He's a tough one, I'm sure we'll find him—alive."

26

*A*ndy carved out a bigger air pocket in front of his face. He'd worn his helmet with the full-face shield down so that gave him a little extra air and probably kept him from certain death with a blow to his head from debris in the slide. He'd need to conserve his oxygen as he worked on his situation. Now his mission was to stay alive long enough to be rescued.

Andy spit in the small air space; it crept down his chin. That gravitational pull told him which way was up and he managed throughout the tumult to keep himself pointed in the right direction. Now he needed to crawl his way to the surface and create enough of an opening for fresh air to reach him. He pushed his elbow down and was able to open up a space to move his hand downward, too. He kept a Bowie knife holstered around his waist and it was imperative to retrieve that. He was relieved to find it still there. In slow, incremental movements he was able to reach the clip on the knife sheath. His glove made it almost impossible to release the clip. He reminded himself to stay calm. He thought about those he left at home, his mom and Emily, as they stood on the porch and waved goodbye. Finally, he succeeded, as he felt the clip and latch loosen.

Andy knew he had to push through his body's limitations in order to survive. He maneuvered his elbow out and back until he thought it safe to draw the knife without an injury to himself. He began the upward drive of the knife blade. Higher and higher, until it passed his face in front of his shield. He stopped to lower his heart rate and recenter his thoughts. His next task was to push the blade up as he rotated it to create a small tunnel in the packed snow. Inch by inch he pressed his arm and the blade toward the life-giving air he desperately needed. When his arm was fully extended, he rested. His other arm had stopped above his head in a reach when the avalanche stopped. He tried to move that hand, but it was numb, as was the arm. He willed the hand to move and grab snow and pull. He visualized the motion but didn't feel it. At the same time, he needed to push his head and body up as far as possible. He moved his helmet up and down, side to side and created bits of space for his shoulders as he scrunched them up and down toward his ears. His muscles cramped and screamed at him. But if he could inch his way upward, he might reach the surface with the tip of his knife. He repeated these movements time after time and stopped to keep his breathing at a minimum. Inch by inch he fought to gain ground against the icy prison. He estimated it to be late evening. It would be a very long night, but he planned to see the morning light. He continued a slow squirm to the surface where he needed to be—sooner than later.

After a time, his left hand was blocked and couldn't move any further. In his struggle Andy had managed over a long period to come within reach of the surface. He'd rested many times to slow his breathing, and lower his heart rate and blood pressure, but his oxygen level had reached a critical stage. He felt overwhelmed with fatigue and fought against his body's craving to shut down and sleep. He was sure that his head would burst from the pain but that seemed to be the only place that he felt actual pain other than cold. He repeated to himself 'one more push—one more time'. And in his last push as he twisted his knife blade, even in his mild stupor, he didn't feel the resistance as he had before. He remained calm and inched himself further upward. And again, he felt less resistance on the knife blade. He questioned if he dared to believe he had reached the surface. With a slow and gradual movement, he pulled his elbow back, enough so as to bring the knife down in front of his face. When his hand cleared the worm hole he breathed deeply and felt the cold of the outside air in his lungs. He had no more strength to move and fell into a deep, exhausted sleep.

*A*ndy startled awake not sure how long he'd slept. The air that came through the hole seemed as cold as earlier, so maybe it hadn't been long. He tried to move up again but something hard pressed on his helmet. As he moved his helmet it seemed to slide evenly, without any kind of uneven resistance. Before he could feel chunks of ice or debris but not now. He raised his knife blade up and moved it at a slight angle. Just past his face, the tip of the knife hit a hard, slick surface. Somehow, he'd come directly up under a chunk of ice. Not knowing how big or wide the obstacle was, he didn't think it wise to try to change his trajectory. At least he had air now and didn't feel any major bodily damage. He'd dressed for much colder temperatures, as he'd factored earlier in the day for the wind chill while on the snow machine, knowing the weather could change in an instant at this location and elevation. In fact, his body was chilled, but his core remained stable enough. The area on his body that felt the coldest was his hands, but the polar dickey mask he'd worn prevented the snow from entering at his neckline and provided an extra layer of warmth.

Andy needed another plan to help the rescuers. He hoped some part of his machine could be seen on the surface, if he was lucky maybe a ski tip or the antenna flag. But reason said the entire thing had been buried. He felt fortunate; at least he'd reached close enough to the surface so he had more air. The pressure of the snow was wearing on him, but he'd stayed in peak physical condition since his return home, so his muscles maintained against the wall of snow and ice that surrounded him.

He knew Sheriff Ben would have the cavalry out in force to search for him. He just needed to keep calm and stay alive.

The snowplows started at 5 a.m. to clear the road from Parsons to the avalanche's path; with four plows on the job it would be completed in an hour. Sheriff Ben made arrangements to get an ambulance in place so Andy could get immediate emergency care. He held the EMTs in high regard as they were on the front line and highly skilled at treating winter victims, especially those who suffered from exposure. He was certain Andy had dressed properly for such an event but wondered if he was hurt or unable to get air. Ben shook his head and pushed those thoughts out of his mind. As far as he was concerned, Andy was alive, and he'd be driving him home soon where he knew Betsy would bake cinnamon rolls on Christmas morning.

Also, at 5 a.m. the search and rescue team formed near the edge of town at the elementary school, where there was plenty of room to stage vehicles, people, sleds and search dogs. There was a large tent erected to provide shelter from the elements, a place to plan and hot drinks with pastries. Even Doc Michaels showed up to attend to Andy.

"Hey, Doc, thanks for coming this morning. I wasn't expecting you, but I appreciate it."

"Well, I felt I needed to here for all the years that Betsy and her boy have helped me.

You just tell me if you need any help from me besides doctoring, okay?"

"Will do, Doc. Hey, there's coffee and donuts over there, help yourself," Ben said and smiled.

Ben stopped and turned. "You know, Doc, it might be a good idea if you rode out with one of the guys. If Andy's seriously hurt, you'd be able to safely get him back here to the ambulance. Is that okay with you?"

"I'm glad you asked, that's a great idea. I brought a big bag with neck brace and such."

"Okay, I'll team you up with one of my men pulling a sled."

At 5:30 a.m. Sheriff Murphy received a call from the local National Guard commander. They would have a bird in the air at 5:50 a.m. from the Avalanche Deployment Unit and be on location above the avalanche site within the hour. However, if wind conditions were deemed too dangerous by the pilot it was upon his discretion to delay or cancel the flight. The air crew would also have the capability for an air rescue if necessary and could be executed with utmost safety. The sheriff would receive constant updated information as the mission moved forward.

Before the sheriff proceeded any further with the search strategy, he called Betsy.

"Good morning, Ben. What's the plan?" Betsy said, her brows pinched.

"Hi, Hon. Well, I have thirty men, snow machines, search dogs and a helicopter going up in about ten minutes. We'll find him, Betsy, I promise you. I'll call as soon as I have him, okay?" Ben tried to be as positive as he could.

"Okay, thanks, Ben. Love you."

"Love you back, Betsy." Ben knew there was nothing more important in his life for him to do. A promise is a promise—especially to the one you love.

Sheriff Ben directed the rescue team members, on a map, to the locations where they needed to be stationed around the base of the avalanche. Two machines also pulled sleds, in which to carry Andy, and were spaced evenly on both sides of the site. All were supplied with radios for communications among themselves and the sheriff, who would drive to a location on the road above, to watch and instruct the search and rescue.

"Remember we're really working against time here. If you spot anything—anything—the smallest detail, you call it in to me. Andy's snow machine is black and green and he's wearing a blue jacket and pants. Be very careful, there's going to be a lot of debris and ice in that snow, too. The slide stripped a few stands of trees, so that's why you'll need to really look closely. The helicopter should fly over in about thirty minutes. If the wind and weather cooperate, we'll have eyes in the sky, too. Any questions? Okay, let's go."

27

When Emily came out of her room, Betsy was seated in a chair by the fireplace. She held a cup with both hands and Lady had her head rested on Betsy's knee. The dog looked up with only her eyes and wagged her tail but didn't move. She had followed Betsy to bed the night before.

"Good morning, Betsy," Emily said, as she bent to give her a hug. She rubbed Lady's ear before she sat down.

"Good morning, Em," Betsy said and looked at Emily seated next to her. "I couldn't sleep last night; this has really made me anxious. I guess because I know he's so close and I can't help him. Sheriff Ben and his men are searching for Andy now. And there's a helicopter on its way, too." Tears formed in her eyes. "I've been here most of the night just praying."

"I'm so sorry, Betsy, I feel helpless, too. But I can't imagine your worry as his mother."

Betsy just stared into the fire. "I set a continental breakfast out for this morning if you're hungry, dear."

"I'll just have some tea for now. Can I get you more tea, too?"

"That would be lovely, thank you." Betsy looked up at Emily as she stood. "Let Cooper know, please, would you?"

Emily shook her head. "Certainly."

As Emily fixed their teas Cooper came downstairs. "Hello, Emily. How are you this morning?" He walked over and gave her a quick kiss and small smile.

"Good morning, Cooper. My body's feeling better each day, thanks. Coffee is made and Betsy set all this out for our breakfast. She's just having tea by the fire and I think I'll join her in there to keep her company."

"Okay, I'll just take my coffee and muffin upstairs. I'm expecting calls, anyway. Talk to you later." Cooper grabbed his breakfast and returned to his room.

Emily sighed, not sure what to think of him—or them.

As she turned to carry the teas into the other room, she heard a phone buzz. She looked around and saw Cooper had forgotten his phone and left it on the counter next to the coffee. The phone was muted so she only heard the vibration and saw it light up. As she walked past the phone she glanced down and saw the name of the caller—Charlotte. Emily sucked in her breath and took a step back. She put the cups down for a moment, as she regained her composure, then continued to her chair to sit with her friend. She heard Cooper come down to retrieve his phone without a word.

*A*ndy rested after he had poked the snow in several places as he tried to find an escape from the ice above him. He had by accident found the only hole through which he'd been able to pierce the surface with his knife blade. He'd achieved his most critical task which was to find air and now he needed to sit and wait to be rescued. He thought, perhaps, he could somehow signal his location. At first, he had an idea he could push his knife out of the hole but, because his head was pinned by a block of ice, he couldn't reach far enough. During his fight to reach the top, his face mask had moved and partially blocked an eye. When he pulled it down, he also grabbed his mother's scarf and it tugged tightly on the side of his neck. He pulled again and thought it felt odd. He grabbed for his jacket collar and something else was there. He worked his fingers around the material and pulled it up in front of his face. He'd forgotten his mother had wrapped her scarf around his neck and tucked it into the top of his jacket. He worked his fingers and hand until he had freed the scarf from around himself and he formulated a new plan. He would try to free the scarf through the air tunnel. If the searchers saw it, they would have an indication of where to send the dogs and he decided it was a good time to give the dogs a more intense scent to detect as he released his bladder.

*B*en stood in the bed of his truck for a better view of his men down below. He was astounded by the magnitude of the avalanche and the ferocity with which it catapulted over the low cliff to the river and valley below. It had been a tidal wave of snow and ice that blasted across the road. The daylight appeared just a few minutes after he arrived, the sky was partly cloudy, and the winds were mild for now. This was their best hope to find Andy and, for once, the weather had cooperated.

As Ben watched, the searchers in the valley fanned out and took their positions at the base of the white behemoth. They got off of their machines almost in unison and waited for further instruction. The handlers had already let the dogs start their search with their noses, when they all heard and saw a military helicopter headed in their direction. The pilot contacted Ben to say the search by air was a go, conditions were favorable. The helicopter began its sweep over the newly formed mountain of snow splayed across a huge swath of the river and valley below Squall Pass.

The light increased and provided the opportunity they needed to mount the ground search. Each member of the team used a snow probe and moved slowly and deliberately as they probed the snowpack and kicked, raked and moved all debris that might have hidden a clue to Andy's location. The dogs sniffed at the edge of the snowpack, back and forth, as they moved little by little uphill. Each man knew the formidable task was worth every effort to save one of their own.

An hour into the hunt the pilot spoke to Sheriff Ben. "I've spotted what appears to be the tip of a ski on a snowmobile." He gave the sheriff directions to its location and Ben passed along the information to the searchers closest to it. Twelve men and a dog rushed to the site, spread out and probed in a systematic pattern. After twenty minutes the dog barked, dug and clawed at a small black, metal object. The men probed, shoveled and uncovered part of Andy's machine. They took great care to probe around the machine as they moved the snow away. But Andy wasn't there. Ben watched with his binoculars from the road and his heart skipped a beat—Andy can't be too far. He studied the path of the avalanche and where the machine had stopped. It appeared Andy had gone in the direction of George and Gracie's house. He calculated the speed of the snow that might have hit Andy and the machine, their weights and the direction. The sheriff had a hunch and he called all of the teams to one area.

Soon the helicopter pilot told Sheriff Murphy that a bright green material had been spotted on the ground stuck to a branch. It flapped in the wind and caught his attention. Ben sent half the team and a dog to the area the pilot gave him. They were close, he knew it, and he knew they needed to hurry.

The first man to reach the new location found a bright,

neon-green neck scarf and waved it high in the air for everyone to see as he yelled. Others arrived and they probed. When the handler and dog got there the dog moved to an area several yards away. It only took a few minutes before the dog barked and dug feverishly. The team moved and probed the area, found the knife tunnel and dug with more excitement. They all called Andy's name and when they uncovered the top of his helmet they yelled and dug harder. When they removed the helmet and face mask, Andy smiled weakly and said, "What took you so long?" Andy took some well-deserved deep breaths. The men worked furiously to get Andy freed from the frozen casket. The team worked in a choreographed motion as they lay him on a thick blanket and lifted him onto a sled. Doc had arrived and braced Andy's neck and did a quick check. He gave a thumbs up with lifted arms that the sheriff saw. Andy's head was covered with a thick wool hat and his entire body covered with one thick wool and two down-filled blankets. He was given some warm water and strapped onto a body-sized plastic sled. Sheriff Ben had asked the helicopter pilot to pick him up and the pilot agreed. The wind had stayed within the margins of safety, so they hovered above and lowered their litter. The men cheered as the helicopter team lifted Andy into safety and flew off to the nearest hospital about thirty minutes flight time away.

The sheriff shook his fist up to the sky and yelled, "Yes. Yes. Yes." He gave instructions to the search and rescue team and got into his truck. He poured a cup of coffee as he wiped away his tears.

As soon as Betsy picked up his call, before she had a chance to say anything, Ben shouted, "We got him, Betsy. Did you hear me? We got him." They both cried out loud and together for several moments.

When they gathered their emotions, Betsy said, "Thank

you, Ben. That's the best Christmas present you've ever given me. Bless you and thank God." She started to quietly sob.

"It's gonna be okay, Betsy, I promise you. The helicopter flew him to Mercy Hospital. I'll go over there now, but I want you to know that Doc Michaels was with Andy and prepped him for the flight. He did a quick check and gave us all a thumbs up."

"Can I go with you, Ben?" Betsy said.

"Not yet, hon, let me take care of my team and all those who helped rescue Andy. I'll call you in about an hour with an update from Doc, he's on his way there now. Take a deep breath, Betsy, and have another cup of tea. Andy might be able to come home today. If so, I'll pick him up. If he has to spend the night, I'll come and get you, okay?"

"Okay, you're the sheriff."

28

*E*mily grinned at Betsy and they both stood in a tight hug as they cried. They released the fear and anxiety which had crept in and almost stolen their hope. Lady knew it was time to celebrate as she danced around the women's legs, barked and wagged her tail.

When they looked at each other Betsy grinned.

"Ben told me to have another cup of tea," she said, through her tears. "He knows me well, doesn't he, Em?"

As the women walked to the kitchen, they felt a lightness and giddiness that accompanied their relief. They sat at the table with their tea and each picked up a muffin from the plate Betsy set on the table.

Emily held up her muffin and said with a grin, "Here's to muffins." Betsy tapped her muffin against the one in the air. The women smiled at each other and before they took a bite, they started to laugh; a deep, healing, joyous laughter which strengthened their weakened spirits.

"Ben will call me in an hour to give me an update, I'll know then if he's taking me to the hospital. That gives me just enough time to get chores done in the barn. I know there's a hungry crew out there," Betsy said. "Would you like to join me?"

"Yes," Emily said, as she shook her head. "I love Noah's Ark." Emily grinned and drank the last of her tea. She noticed when she sat down at the table that Lady again rested near her chair. "I think Lady knows I'm the one that needs attention now."

"That girl knows more than any of us ever will. She amazes me often."

As the women walked out of the front door, Emily heard Cooper's voice upstairs.

*A*s Betsy and Emily fed the animals, they talked about the two rescues and how fragile life is.

"I never take a day for granted, you know, Em. We aren't promised tomorrow, so you need to hold your partner close, show them and tell them what they mean to you and how much you love them," Betsy said and then grinned. "Besides, it's great exercise for your heart, it never wears out and the warranty never expires." Betsy chuckled.

Emily laughed. "I didn't think about it that way. That's a great perspective and credo to live by, thanks. I hope I'm as happy in my relationship as you and Hank were."

"Don't get me wrong, a marriage does take constant work, but like a garden well-tended, the abundance of the harvest is worth it. Your partnership has been cultivated daily. You just have to identify the weeds and keep them pulled out. And understand the weeds are always just under the surface waiting for the opportunity to sprout. So, you take care not to feed and water where you know they'll grow. And once any sprout, you pull them before they can drop their roots deep, take the food from the soil and block the sun from the plants that are important. If you don't do that they'll overtake and choke out what you're really trying to grow."

Emily threw more feed to the chickens as she listened and processed Betsy's words. She nodded in agreement. "Yeah, I only want the flowers and the vegetables to grow. I guess you have to get tired of the weeds in your life, don't you?" Emily's face was pensive. The chickens squawked and flapped their wings because she had stopped feeding them. "Oops, sorry my feathered followers." Emily chuckled. "I don't think they appreciate my technique. I probably won't get any applause or rave reviews today." She snickered and grabbed a handful of the seeds and tossed them into the air. She watched as they pecked furiously and scrambled to eat everything before another could. "You know, Betsy, I look at those chickens and I can relate to them. I'm pretty sure that's what my life has become by living in the city. People walk all over others to get the best or the most. I'm not sure that's what I want for my life. It might be time for a change." Emily put the bucket down just as Betsy finished feeding Max.

"I think I'll have another cup of tea and wait for Ben's call. Sound good to you?"

As the women went into the house Emily commented how wonderful it felt to see the sun again.

"You know, Betsy, I'm going to apply your words starting today. The sun is shining, and I appreciate its warmth on my face, so I won't dwell on the clouds and snow that are on the way." Emily grinned and they laughed.

Betsy had almost finished her tea, as they sat by the fire, when her phone rang. "Hi, Ben, how's my boy?" Betsy said cautiously.

"Well, as a matter of fact, I'm standing right beside him and he wants to talk to you. Hold on, Betsy."

"Hi, Mom, how are you?" Andy laughed, then grew silent. "Mom? Are you there? Hello?"

Betsy wiped her tears and gained her composure. "It's so

good to hear your voice, Andy." Her voice cracked as she whispered, "I love you so much."

"And I love you very much, too, Mom. When I was buried, I kept thinking about you and Emily as you stood on the porch to say goodbye as I left. I'm so sorry I worried you. But do you remember what I said to you yesterday morning, Mom? I promised I'd come home. And you and Dad taught me to always keep my promises, especially to those you love."

"Thank you, Andy. You're right, you have always kept your promises," Betsy said, as she smiled. "My heart is full today."

"So, Doc Michaels is here, too, making sure I'm well taken care of. I'm just dehydrated and tired, no frostbite. My new gear worked wonders to keep me warm. But did Ben tell you what the miracle was? Your green scarf you wrapped around my neck is what I used to signal my location. I guess it started to blow away but got caught on a branch close to me. I'm living proof of the hope that exists on Glimmer Mountain." Andy had tears in his eyes but joy in his voice. "I just need to be here a few more hours for observation but I'm pretty sure Ben will be able to bring me home then. I'm so ready for some of your cooking, Mom."

"I can hardly wait to wrap my arms around you, son. You may be a grown man but there's a place in my heart where a little boy still lives. I'll put a roast in the oven for you right now, I know that's your favorite just like your dad. I was saving it for Christmas Day, but I do believe Christmas came early this year." Betsy smiled and sighed.

"Sounds fantastic, Mom. Okay, I'll give this back to Ben. Bye, I love you." Andy smiled as he spoke and wiped the tears away.

"I'll bring your boy home safe and sound, Betsy, and I'll call when I'm on my way. I love you. Bye."

"I love you, too, Ben. Thanks, and I'm expecting you to stay for supper with us. Bye."

*B*etsy turned to Emily with a huge smile. "He's going to be fine and Ben will bring him home by dinner time. I'll put a roast in the oven and then I'm going to take a quick nap, I'm exhausted. That couch over there just might be calling your name," Betsy said. "You should rest, Em, I know this has been hard on you, too." Betsy gave Emily a quick peck on the cheek as she walked past.

"Yeah, that does sound like a good idea. I'll find a book in the library, a boring book," Emily said, as she giggled. She stood and stretched, then realized she could move her ribs much better even than yesterday. And she was certain the relief brought by the good news helped.

Betsy busied herself in the kitchen with a cacophony of pots, pans and the silverware drawer as she hurried. When her task was completed, with a prime rib roast in the oven, she left to her room, where she needed to give a very special thank you.

Emily walked to the library but, as always, was drawn first to the magnificent view from the windows. She was surprised at her good luck; the deer were just crossing the meadow again. She was fascinated by them and the simplicity of their lives. She clung to that pristine vision even as the worry and heaviness of heart pulled her thoughts away. Lost in the celebration of Andy's return was the memory of that early morning call—from Charlotte.

29

*E*mily stood in front of the window and stared at her reflection. The world outside had disappeared and her doubts and fear crashed into her moment of tranquility. She knew very little about Charlotte, only that Cooper told her she was his previous girlfriend and it just didn't work out. At the time he told her that much, he seemed dismissive of the relationship. It seemed to her that it hadn't been serious, and she had no further thoughts about Charlotte. The only reason Cooper said anything about her to begin with was because Mrs. Hamilton had made reference to their having been together before Emily entered the picture. Emily was rankled by the thought of Mrs. Hamilton.

Emily stood there for twenty minutes more and sighed deeply. She had a mild headache, but it was nothing compared to the pounding of her heart. She decided she should ask Cooper about Charlotte's call. He had been in such a foul mood since being here that she felt this would not go well. But she needed to ask.

Emily took a deep breath as she lifted her chest and squared her shoulders, which was much easier done than six days ago. It was time to confront Cooper about Charlotte and she wanted all the details. She remembered how fondly his mother had spoken her name in just that brief conversation.

When Emily turned, she was shocked by Cooper as he walked toward her and her eyes widened. He kissed her as she walked to a chair and sat down.

"Did they find Andy?" Cooper said, as he sat, his face unemotional.

His question surprised her. "Yes. Yes, they did and he's okay. They airlifted him to a hospital for observation, but Sheriff Ben will bring him home in a few hours if all goes well." Emily gave him a weak smile.

"That's good news, I'm sure Betsy is relieved. Is she resting?"

Emily nodded her head. "We'll get all the details at dinner tonight. Betsy has a special meal planned in honor of his safe rescue and return."

"I'll be there for sure. Do you know if the road has been cleared yet?" Cooper asked.

"Oh, I almost forgot to tell you. Yes, it's been cleared all the way to Parsons and all connecting roads are good for at least another twenty-four hours. The sheriff told Betsy another big storm is expected late tomorrow."

"That gives us a day to get out of here and on to Hamilton House. Finally," Cooper said with a loud exhalation. "I'll call my father and tell him he can send a car for us. I'm so ready to be back in civilization where I can properly take care of business. So far, I've been able to manage but much longer and it would be chaos. That could've cost me a ton of money."

As Cooper stood, Emily rose and grabbed his arm to stop him from leaving. "Cooper, I need to talk to you about something that has upset me. I want complete honesty, please, don't leave out any information." Emily said, as she hesitated.

"If I'm going to believe in our future then, I need to believe in the past."

Cooper turned to face her about four feet away. "Okay, go ahead, Emily."

"This morning as I walked by your phone, which you'd forgotten on the kitchen counter, it buzzed, and I noticed the caller's name was Charlotte. Is she the same woman you dated before me? And why has she called you now?" Emily's heart pounded as if to rip out of her chest.

"Oh, that," Cooper said, in a nonchalant tone. "Mother has invited her to join us at a dinner and she called to ask if it would be acceptable with me. Which I responded that her presence made no difference to me. I was involved with someone else now and that's that."

Emily knew that wasn't the entire story. Her gut told her as much, so she persisted. "You told me the two of you had only dated briefly. Just how long were you together that she's concerned how you would feel about seeing her again?"

Cooper's countenance changed to annoyance. "You're making a big deal out of nothing, Emily. She's history. Leave it at that." His face hardened and his eyes narrowed.

"How often have you spoken to her since we've been together? Do you still care for her? I think the two of you were way more than you're willing to say. You act like you're guarding a secret. And if you're talking to this former girl-friend and have nothing to hide, wouldn't you, out of respect for me, share that with me rather than taking the chance I'd find out some other way. Besides, I'm sure your mother would happily share that information with me. I know she thinks any former girlfriend would be better for you than me."

Cooper chose another tact and softened his tone and face. "Yes, we were engaged but I didn't think the information was important enough to tell you. You are who I want, Emily. It's you I think about and want to give everything to. Charlotte doesn't hold a place in my heart anymore. Believe me, trust me—it's only you. I love you." Cooper stepped forward and took Emily's hand. "I think we have a future together and it would make me happy."

Emily was confused and maybe she'd overreacted. She had been upset and maybe she overthought everything, but still, there was a feeling and gnawing doubt she found hard to put aside. But this wasn't the place or time to have a further discussion about Cooper and Charlotte. Although, there was something about his mannerism when he spoke about her.

*E*mily talked with Betsy as she prepared dinner. Ben had called and told her Andy would be home in about an hour.

"It will be so good to see Andy. It seems like a lifetime since he's been gone," Emily said, as she sipped her tea. She giggled and said, "And I feel like I've lived here for a lifetime. You're so easy to talk to and be with, Betsy. It's going to be hard to leave." Emily's smile turned into a frown.

"Then don't," Betsy said, as she smiled. "You are always welcome here, Em, really, I mean it. You've become family as far as I'm concerned. Lady thinks so, too." Betsy giggled.

Lady was beside Emily's chair as she rubbed her ear. "I think I'll put her in my suitcase." Emily laughed and looked down at Lady who made eye contact. "I swear it feels like she looks into my soul when she does that."

"Maybe she is," Betsy chuckled. "So, are you and Cooper on the mend from the other day?" Betsy turned to look at Emily with concern on her face.

"I guess so, it's hard to tell," Emily said in a sad voice.

"I don't know that much about your relationship or Cooper, but you deserve to be happy, Em. Does he do that for you?" Betsy turned to face Emily.

"Yes, most of the time. He's been really pressured lately so he's distracted and kind of moody. But if he's ever cross with me or too busy to be with me, he'll give me a nice present. See, he gave these diamond earrings to me on the way here. Which now seems forever ago. But he is generous."

"It looks like Cooper can give you everything he thinks your heart desires. But is that what you desire, Em?" Betsy stopped stirring and looked at Emily with kindness in her eyes. "Just remember only you know what makes you happy. And I truly wish you to be happy."

"Thank you, Betsy, for your concern and words of wisdom and encouragement. They mean a lot to me." Emily smiled. "And, by the way, this does feel like home."

"Good, that means a lot to me." Betsy smiled and winked. "Set the table for me, please?"

Emily turned as she heard Cooper's footsteps. He gave her a quick kiss as he walked past.

"I heard the good news, Betsy, I'm happy for you," Cooper said as he smiled at Betsy.

"Yes, thank you. It's time to celebrate so we're having Christmas dinner early." Betsy's laugh was filled with relief and joy. "I hope you brought an appetite down with you, Cooper. It's going to be a feast."

"I certainly did. It's hard work conquering the world." He smiled and looked at Emily.

"Did Emily tell you we'll be leaving tomorrow? Father is sending a car for us. I can't thank you enough for your hospitality, Betsy."

"Yes, she did. But I wish it wasn't so soon. The house will be so empty without you both here. But I know you'll be glad to spend Christmas at your parents' house," Betsy said.

"Actually, we usually have dinner at the country club; that's been our tradition since I was small. My father would rather skip the holiday because it interferes with business. And my mother has the staff decorate; she's really just interested in shopping for herself." Cooper chuckled. "Father says it makes her happy and that's what Christmas is all about, right?"

Betsy glanced at Emily's fallen expression and held up a spoon. "Here, taste this, Em."

$\mathcal{L}$ady jumped up from beside Emily's chair. She ran to the front door and barked and jumped wildly.

"Wow, the boys must be coming up the driveway." Betsy smiled and laughed. "I haven't seen her that excited in a long time. Well, I'm pretty excited, too, I must admit. Okay, Lady, let's go greet them."

Emily and Cooper followed Betsy across the room and when Betsy opened the door Sheriff Ben and Andy had just gotten out of the truck. Betsy ran down the stairs and threw her arms around Andy's neck. He hugged her tightly for several minutes.

"Okay, Mom, we need to go in the house now. Remember me? I'm the one who suffered from exposure." Andy threw his head back and laughed.

"Oh, yes—yes, of course. But don't be surprised if I put a lot more headlocks on you tonight," Betsy said, as she laughed.

"Trust me, Mom, I'll welcome them." Andy looked at his mother with such love and tears in his eyes.

Betsy led them all into the house, Sheriff Ben close behind her. As Andy passed Emily, they locked eyes and she said,

"I'm so very happy that you're home and well. You had us scared." She smiled. "And, by the way, you missed the peach cobbler," Emily said, as she winked.

Cooper stood several feet away and watched Emily's face as she spoke to Andy. His jaws tightened and he moved closer to put his arm around her waist. "Yes, you're fortunate they found you in time." Cooper's eyes narrowed as he almost smiled.

Andy caught the slight change on Cooper's face and knew what he really meant. But Andy was not intimidated by this wealthy playboy. "It's good to see you, too, Coop." Andy grinned his crooked smile at him and then back at Emily. He strode into the kitchen.

"I hope the food's ready because I sure am and I'm sitting down at the table right now." Andy clapped his hands twice and spread his arms as he shouted, "Bring the dinner, woman." He looked fondly at Betsy and they laughed.

"Let me help you, Betsy," Ben said with a smile.

"No, you go sit down. Heroes don't have to help." She gave him a quick kiss on the cheek. "And you are my hero, Ben." They exchanged warm smiles before Ben walked to the table and sat down.

As Betsy set the prime rib on the table, Ben laughed and said, "Is this from the fattened calf?" He swept his hand and arm toward Andy. "Your prodigal has returned." The men had a great laugh as Betsy swiped Ben on the shoulder as she giggled. Emily laughed but Cooper didn't understand the joke.

Andy and Ben related their stories of a harrowing ordeal and heroes at large. They shared how their camaraderie with the town's people was such a special bond and support for all who lived on the mountain. They lived in harmony and agreement and friendship. If one fell another was there to pick them up. They shared in their joys and their grief. It was a kinship of love and respect for each other—a sense of belonging.

$\mathcal{A}$ndy pushed his chair back and stood. "Mom, that meal was amazing, as always. Thank you." He reached to pick up his plate and Betsy gently slapped his hand.

"Nope. I want you to go sit by the fire and prop your legs up. I'll bring cake to you. You too, Ben."

Andy laughed and hugged her. "Okay, you're the boss. And that fire is something I sure could have used twenty-four hours ago." Andy grinned and walked to the living room.

"I'd love to, Betsy, but I need to get back to the office. There's still tons of paperwork and phone calls I need to make," the sheriff said, as he stood and walked to the door.

"I suppose so," said Betsy. "I'll save some dessert for you. Are you coming back in the morning to spend Christmas Eve and Christmas day with us, as usual?"

"Absolutely, I wouldn't miss it for the world, you know that." Ben reached down to give Betsy a hug and felt something in his coat pocket. He handed her a bundle of letters. "Oh, here, I brought your mail that had piled up while the road was closed."

Betsy took the mail and set it on the small table by the door. "Be careful and drive safe going back to town, Ben. For me, okay?" She gave him a quick hug and waved from the porch. She and Lady watched as the taillights faded into the darkness. She rubbed a furry ear and sighed. "It's warmer inside don't you think, Lady?"

Andy had already eaten some cake and was asleep on the couch. Lady sniffed his face and then took her position by Emily. Betsy covered Andy with a soft blanket and kissed his forehead. She looked over and saw that there was tea and cake set by her chair. She whispered a thank you to Emily.

"He couldn't wait," Emily said, as she smiled at Betsy. "I brought cake in for us and his was gone in about three bites. He said he just needed a warm nap by the fireplace."

Betsy sat down by Emily. "Thanks for getting that for him. I can't imagine how exhausted he must be." She looked at Andy breathing heavily. "You know, Em, he's just like his father. Hank served in the military for eight years, war time years. He won medals but never talked about them, just like Andy. They are brave, tough men but with great, big hearts. Andy is all heart, always has been. It's wonderful for those around him, but that means he has so much more to be broken. He's only had one serious relationship and she sent him a Dear John letter while he was on tour. It took years for him to get over it. I think my war hero is afraid to love again. I pray he finds someone and has a partnership like his father and I did." Betsy sighed, smiled at Emily and took a bite of her cake.

The women watched the fire for a while and sipped their tea as they reflected on the events of the last few days.

Emily set her empty cup down and looked at Betsy and her eyes twinkled.

"I think Sheriff Murphy is kind of sweet on you," Emily giggled.

"Oh Ben? He's had a crush on me since I don't know, forever, I guess. But when you get to be my age a really close friendship is better than a maybe romance. I know he's always there for me, he was Hank's best friend. And he gave me a shoulder to lean on when Hank died. But me and the sheriff, we have a closer friendship than most married folks. We both know there's no one for me after Hank. But when Ben gets sick, I take him chicken soup. And if my truck gets stuck, he's mad at me if I don't call him." Betsy chuckled. "We share our memories of Hank and that sustains us. I think Ben loved Hank almost as much as me. Sometimes I'd hear them bickering and say they sounded like an old married couple. It's rare to have a friend like that. Besides, we like to argue about who's memory is better, his or mine." Both women laughed.

"And I agree, that dinner was simply beyond delicious. Recipe?" Emily giggled.

"Of course, Em, any time. You need to leave your contact information for me, please. That way we can stay in touch and I can send a recipe book to you." They both giggled. Betsy stood, too, and walked to the laundry room. She had forgotten to fold the clean towels.

31

*E*mily set her suitcase on the bed and packed most of her clothes. She wasn't quite sure what she would wear the next day. While she thought about it, she went upstairs to ask Cooper when the car would be there to pick them up. As she raised her hand to knock on Cooper's door, she heard him on the phone.

"We'll be there about midday tomorrow. I'll be happy to see you, too. Yes, Emily's fine. Yes, Mother, I have the ring. I know, I know she's not your first choice. But then Father said I needed a wife before he introduced me as the new vice president of the company. Ask Father, he'll explain it again if that's what will convince you. I don't have time to find someone else and have a long courtship. Besides, she's a sweet girl and I know she loves me, not my money, like those other women you introduced me to. Emily will do just fine. I love her enough and I'm sure that will grow over time. She's very intelligent and I'm sure you'll be able to teach her the social skills she needs to be part of our family."

Horrified, Emily backed away from the door. Cooper's words echoed and repeated over and over in her head. 'Emily will do. Love her enough.' She stood in the hallway, frozen and wide-eyed. She faced in the direction of his voice, as if she could see him. She didn't hear the footsteps behind her on the wooden stairs.

As Betsy topped the stairs, she saw Emily and asked, "Hi, did you need something, dear?"

Emily only turned her head toward Betsy, her face pale as her hands shook. The meaning of Cooper's words had processed, and she bolted past Betsy and down the stairs.

Frightened, Betsy dropped the towels and rushed back down the stairs as she called after Emily. "Em—Emily, what's wrong?" But Emily ran down the stairs, through the house and was already out of the front door as it slammed against the wall. She ran out into the night without her coat and only slippers on her feet.

Cooper heard Betsy call for Emily, but it got quiet, so he continued his conversation with Mrs. Hamilton not knowing the chain of events his words set into motion.

Andy woke up when he heard the commotion. He sat up and looked across the room in time to see Emily run out of the door. He knew something was terribly wrong and called out her name. He grabbed his coat as he hurried to slip his feet into his boots. Lady had dashed out the door in pursuit of Emily, too.

Andy ran outside, down the stairs, then stood still. He heard her sobs and the crunching of the icy snow. He also heard Lady as she whined.

"Emily," he shouted, as he ran in the direction of the weeping sounds. "Emily." Andy was panicked.

Emily heard her name shouted out as the darkness enveloped her. She was numb to the cold that bit her skin and the snow caked on her feet. She ran toward the road without thought; she needed distance from Cooper. After several minutes her body refused to continue the pace. She slowed to a walk and realized she'd been crying, and she began to shiver. She felt so betrayed, so alone. Then she heard Andy's voice.

"Emily, where are you? Emily, please, come back. Whatever it is, I'll help you. I promise. Just call out my name. Lady, come here." Andy pleaded and strained to see in the darkness.

"Andy, I'm here," she said in a quiet voice. And a moment later he was by her side. He took off his coat, wrapped it around her, then just as quickly lifted her into his arms. He walked her silently back to the house. She rested her head against his chest—she could hear his heartbeat. It quieted her fear and her tears stopped.

Betsy met them at the door. Before she could speak, Andy shook his head at her. She said nothing as Andy carried Emily to the living room. Betsy grabbed the blanket on the couch and watched as Andy took care of their guest.

"Here, sit by the fire, you're freezing. I don't need to know what happened, but I do need to get you warm." Andy put her in an armchair and pushed it closer to the fireplace. Betsy handed him the blanket which he draped over Emily's body and legs. He tucked the blanket around her as she sat motionless. He grabbed a pillow from the couch, set it on the hearth, and placed her feet on it. Then he turned and looked at her. The anguish on her face was obvious and he felt the anger grow in the pit of his stomach. He could tell the pain was related to her heart—and to Cooper. He fought the urge to climb the stairs and confront him, but he knew it wasn't his place. Instead, he walked to the kitchen and brought back a steaming cup of cocoa and handed it to her.

"Use this to warm your hands, Em." He sat on the floor next to her chair as he stroked Lady's head. He sighed as he looked at her as she stared at the fire.

They said nothing. And that was okay.

❄

*E*mily stopped shivering and had finished her cocoa. The warmth had returned to her body, but she felt sad and confused. She looked at Andy and Lady beside her. He had fallen asleep with his head and arm on her chair and his hand on Lady. Lady lifted her eyes to look at Emily but didn't move her head.

Emily looked at the Christmas tree and studied the lights as they twinkled. When she was a child, she would spend hours watching the lights and waiting for Christmas day. She really missed her mom and dad. She stood up, careful not to disturb Andy. She touched the bell and it rang in a clear, quiet tone and her fingers tingled. She wondered what could cause that.

Her question went unanswered as she felt Andy stand beside her. This time she took the bell from the tree and Andy touched it. It rang louder and more harmonious than ever before, as her hand tingled and her heart fluttered. Her eyes widened and she looked up at Andy.

"Did you feel that? Or is it my imagination." Emily said. She hung the bell back on the tree as it continued to ring for several more seconds.

"Yeah, I'm not sure what that was." Andy said, with a puzzled look.

Emily moved closer to the fireplace and Andy followed her. They stood with their backs to the fire. Her face still mirrored her sadness.

"Thank you, Andy." Emily didn't want to share her heartbreak with anyone.

"I'll be there for you any time you need me. I promise," Andy said as he gently moved a little wavy strand of hair from the side of her eye.

"I should pack and go to bed. You need to sleep, too, Andy. I'm sorry I woke you." Emily gave him a pained smile.

"It's okay, I can sleep any time. And anywhere. Even in

snow." Andy gave her his crooked smile. "You're what's important, Em. And don't ever, ever forget that. Okay?"

Emily nodded her head. "Good night, Andy."

"Good night, Em." Andy's eyes teared as he watched her walk away.

*B*etsy had seen that her son would take good care of Emily, so she went to bed. She knew her son and she knew how broken his heart would be tomorrow. But when she saw him carry Emily into the house it brought back a memory. She had fallen and sprained her ankle years before, and Hank had whisked her up in his arms and carried her into the house. He put her on the couch and elevated her leg on a pillow. He then came back with an ice bag to stop the swelling. The next time he came back, he handed her a bouquet of handpicked wildflowers. He had taken such good care of her and her heart— always.

She would be sad to see Emily leave and she knew Andy would be even more sad. She had a suspicion about Emily being so upset. Betsy had clearly heard Cooper's conversation a few days before just outside his door. She said a prayer for Emily and those she loved. She touched the corner of the frame that held Hank's picture before she turned off the lamp.

*E*mily finished packing and decided to take a hot bath. She sunk into the water and thought about Cooper's words. She knew Mrs. Hamilton frustrated him, she heard that in his voice. He probably didn't mean what he said, or she didn't hear him correctly. His father put a lot of pressure on him and he was trying to appease them both. She'd ask Cooper tomorrow on the way to Hamilton House. And she had been through a lot of trauma herself this past week, maybe she was too emotional and overreacted. Her body was thoroughly warmed as she crawled into bed and fell asleep.

*A*ndy lay in bed unable to sleep despite the fatigue from the night before. He was furious at Cooper and that told him to what extent his heart had already begun to fall in love with Emily. He'd only just met her, but it was much more than her beauty, her outward appearance and more than her intelligence. She had a compassionate heart and a joy for life and laughter, something he had not found in another.

She was so weary and sad when he brought her back into the house, that he wanted to hold her, as they stood at the fireplace, but she wasn't his to hold. He wanted to comfort and protect her from injury to her heart or body. He wanted—but she was not his to want.

32

*E*arly the next morning Betsy cooked the annual Christmas Eve breakfast. Hank loved Eggs Benedict with homemade hollandaise sauce, but he wanted to keep it special, so he decided to only have it once a year. Betsy would also serve Belgian waffles, with strawberries from her garden and whipped cream, orange-glazed ham slices, honey-sage sausage patties, southern home fries and fresh blueberry coffee cake.

Emily was the first one to the kitchen and she had a big smile.

"Whatever all this is, please, put it in the recipe book," Emily laughed and inhaled deeply.

"Good morning, Em," Betsy said and smiled. "I hope you're hungry. Would you set the table, please?"

"Sure, I can do that. It would be a pleasure."

"I haven't seen either of the guys yet. Hopefully, they'll show up soon."

As her words still hung in the air, Andy came around the corner with a big smile.

"As if I'd miss your world-famous Christmas Eve breakfast, Mom," Andy teased. He walked over and kissed the cook on the cheek.

"Did you sleep well, Andy?" Betsy said, as she looked him up and down to check that he had nothing missing. "I'm surprised you're up so early after your adventure in the woods."

"Adventure?" Andy said in a mocking tone. He looked at Emily and grinned. She grinned back as she continued to set the table.

Emily heard Cooper come down the stairs. He walked over to her and gave her a kiss on the cheek.

"Good morning everyone." Cooper seemed to be in a good mood. "That smells really good, Betsy."

"Well, we're all here so let's eat," Betsy said, with plates of food in her hands.

Andy helped carry the last of the platters to the table and they were all seated.

"I bet you're anxious to get back to reality, aren't you, Coop?" Andy said, and smiled congenially as he passed the ham. He struggled not to expose the hostility he felt, for Emily's sake. Cooper seemed clueless to last night's drama and Emily was in a good mood as well. Andy decided he'd need to talk with his mother after their guests left.

"Cooper, I forgot to ask you last night what time the car will be here to pick us up." Emily glanced up as she took a bite of waffle.

"I spoke with Father this morning. Arthur left early, so he should be here by one o'clock, if not earlier. Is your bag packed?"

"Yes, of course. I packed last night." Emily's brow knitted slightly, but she smiled.

"Well, we can enjoy this wonderful meal and the company at leisure. I only have a few calls to make, then it should be time to go," Cooper said, as he smiled at everyone.

As the last person finished, Cooper excused himself and went upstairs.

Emily and Andy helped clear the table as Betsy put the leftovers away.

"That's good, Andy, Em and I can finish in here. We have more girl talk to get done before she leaves," Betsy said and grinned. "Oh, I just remembered, Ben gave me a bundle of mail before he left, and I set it by the door. Would you get that for me, please?"

Andy retrieved the bundle and handed it to his mom. She rifled through it and pulled a large envelope out. "Here, this is for you. It's from Angela."

*A*ndy took the envelope to the library and sat at his desk. He opened it and found another envelope and a Christmas card inside. He opened the card first.

"Dear Andy,

Willie gave me instructions to send this to you on the second Christmas after his death. Christina and I are doing well. We love you and wish you a very Merry Christmas and Happy New Year. —Love, Angela"

Andy looked at the other envelope. It was addressed to him in Willie's messy handwriting. He'd always teased Willie about his scribbling. Andy took a breath and held it for several seconds. His hands trembled as he opened the second envelope. Inside was a neatly folded letter. Andy pulled out the paper and unfolded it. It read:

"Hey, Buddy,

Yeah, we know I'm dead if you're reading this. But it happens to all of us sooner or later. For you, I hope it's much later because you promised to watch after Angela and my baby, Christina. They were everything to me. And it's too bad I won't be there to watch my baby grow up or to grow old with my Angela. I know you'll take good care of them because you always kept your promises. Thanks!

Now for you, there was nothing else you could have done, Andy. It wasn't in the cards for me to be here. I've known you since we were kids and you always had my back. So stop feeling guilty, let it go, man. The best thing you can do now, to honor me, is to live your life to the fullest. Live it for both of us. Find a gorgeous woman and have lots of babies. You deserve to be happy. You're the best friend any man could have asked for. Merry Christmas, Andy, and have a Happy New Year. —Willie"

Tears rolled down Andy's face as he read the letter a second and third time. As he cried, years of agony and guilt were washed away. He and Willie were closer than brothers and Willie knew him like no one else. They had shared all the good and the bad life threw at them. They had been honest with each other. Andy sighed. "Man, I miss you, Willie. Thank you," Andy said out loud, as he put the letter in his desk.

$\mathcal{W}$hile the ladies visited for the last time and cleaned the kitchen, Betsy's phone rang.

"Well, good morning, Sheriff Murphy," Betsy said and giggled.

Ben laughed. Betsy had a way of doing that to him. She was a beautiful human being. "Good morning, Betsy, how's our boy this morning?"

"He seems to be doing well after a long sleep and big breakfast. He's reading his mail."

"I'm so thankful we found him. You know what you can give me for Christmas?" Ben asked. "A bright green scarf," Ben said and laughed.

"I'd be happy to. I don't want to lose you either." Betsy smiled and laughed.

"Hey, just calling to let you know I'm on my way. Need anything?"

"Nope, just you, Ben. I'll have a plate ready for you. I love you. Bye."

"Love you, too. Bye, Betsy." Ben smiled and sighed, contentment on his face.

As Betsy put the phone down, Andy walked into the kitchen. His eyes were red from the cry, but he wore a huge, crooked smile.

"Andy, what's happened? Are Angela and Christina alright?" Betsy said, concerned.

"Yes, Angela and the baby are doing fine."

"Are you okay then?" Betsy's face still looked worried.

"I'm more than okay, Mom, my debt is paid. I've been released." The joy on his face reflected a new, inner peace she hadn't seen since his return. She said a prayer of thanks.

Emily wondered what had changed Andy. It was almost as if his countenance glowed. Betsy understood, as only a mother could. Whatever happened she was happy for him.

The next moment Cooper entered as he carried his suitcase. He seemed anxious to make his departure. He smiled and was more congenial at breakfast than he'd been all week.

"Emily, is your suitcase ready? I'll take it to the door," Cooper said, almost jovial.

"Yes, it's packed. Leave the smaller bag, though, I'll take that," Emily said.

Cooper turned and walked to the door, where he left his bag, and then went to Emily's room to retrieve hers. His phone rang and he returned to his bedroom, one last time.

"Em, let's have another tea by the fire. And a little more girl talk before you have to go." Betsy smiled but her heart was already missing her new companion.

"Sounds good to me," Emily said, and brought the cups to the counter.

Their conversation was light and full of the memories they had made in such a short time. When Ben arrived, Betsy filled a plate and sat him at the table. Andy sat with him to recount his harrowing experience and again praised him for finding him. Betsy rejoined Emily next to the fire.

"I'll really miss you, Betsy," Emily paused, "and this fire." Both women giggled.

"I know Andy now has a deeper appreciation for it." Betsy smiled and winked. "I'll miss you, too, Em. You've been a breath of fresh air for my soul and this house. It will feel so much emptier without your laughter." Betsy's eyes welled up as she smiled at Emily.

The women sat in silence and finished their tea as they basked in the fire's warmth.

33

"*E*mily, the car will be here in five minutes. Are you ready to go?" Cooper said, excitement in his voice. He hadn't enjoyed his stay at Betsy's B&B, as his father would take every opportunity to remind him of his failed plan.

"Yes, Cooper, I'm ready." The women stood and looked each other in the eyes. They reached out and embraced, a long hug filled with love.

As they hugged, Betsy whispered in Emily's ear, "Whenever you need an answer, Em, God is only a breath away."

Emily gasped at the words she heard. Her mother had quoted that to her often.

"Emily, the car is here," Cooper said. He shook hands with both men and thanked them. Betsy stood by the door and Cooper gave her a short hug and repeated his words of gratitude. He grabbed the suitcases and set them outside as they all walked onto the porch.

"Sheriff Ben, it's been a pleasure to meet you and share some time together," Emily said, as she tiptoed to hug him.

Ben leaned down with a sincere smile on his face. "The pleasure was all mine, Emily. Have a Merry Christmas and Happy New Year, hon."

Emily turned to Andy and they smiled. Their eyes locked and as they hugged, Cooper walked to the bottom of the stairs.

"Emily, it's time to go. Are you ready?" Cooper's tone and face showed his irritation.

Emily turned to Cooper and her smile faded.

"Yes, Cooper, I am ready," Emily said, her voice clear and stern. "I'm ready to tell you I won't be going with you. I've decided I never want to see you again or step another foot into Hamilton House." Emily looked at Cooper with eyes fixed.

"What do you mean? We were fine before we landed here." Cooper's eyes cut to Andy.

"I heard your conversation with your mother last night and I know why you really want me in your life. You are a manipulator and you disgust me." Emily stepped down two stairs and stood face to face with Cooper. She could hear him breathe as she stood tall and tilted her chin up.

The shock of Emily's epithet caused Cooper's mouth to gape open. His stunned look and his lack of words spoke volumes of his guilt. He had no response.

"It's a shame you never played chess, especially with me." Emily glowered at Cooper. "I choose not to be your pawn, Cooper. And you might need to ask someone what this means," she said, as she sneered at him. "You'll have to capture the queen without my help. Good luck. And goodbye."

It was evident that Emily's words stung Cooper's ego. His face grew red, his features hardened, and his eyes narrowed. She had humiliated him in front of an audience. No one had ever done that to him, not even Charlotte. He said nothing and as he turned and walked toward the waiting car, he reached into his pocket and brought out his phone. He pressed the call button, stopped and turned to look at Emily.

"Hello, Charlotte, it seems I'm once again available."

Cooper got into the car and closed the door. Lady barked and chased the vehicle for several yards before she returned with ears up as she wagged her tail. She sat in front of Emily and looked up at her as Emily reached down and rubbed a furry ear. "Good girl, Lady, you wonderful guard dog."

The group watched Cooper as his driver pulled away. Emily smiled and held out her hands to Betsy and Andy, who stood beside her, and they gripped her hands. Betsy reached out to Ben, he took her hand and stood closer to his friend. They were silent until the car was out of sight.

Emily sighed and took a long breath of the cool air. She felt the burden lifted and her spirit set free again.

"Andy, how would you like to lose at a game of chess?" Emily's smile was met by Andy's smile and then a crooked grin. The enormity of her words made his pulse quicken, his eyes widen and for a moment he held his breath.

"Is that a challenge?" Andy said. As Emily nodded her head, Andy grabbed her around the waist, and she wrapped her arms around his neck. He swung her around once, as she giggled, before he gently set her down.

34

"*A*nyone else need more blueberry coffee cake?" Emily said and laughed as she grabbed Andy's hand and pulled him into the house and toward the kitchen.

Andy laughed and grinned. "I do," he said, "and maybe another waffle." The two laughed as they got more plates and cups. As they scooped the blue-marbled cake onto the small plates, Andy's joy was evident and Emily's face glowed.

As Betsy and Ben walked into the dining area, she turned to him with a huge grin and chuckled. "I hope those are your dancing shoes, Sheriff, because I'll be watching as you two-step down Main Street." She threw her head back and burst out laughing as they walked into the kitchen.

Ben grinned, grabbed Betsy's hand and spun her around. "And I think you'll be my dance partner, Betsy." He spun her again and they all laughed.

"That wasn't part of the deal, Ben." Betsy giggled.

❄

*E*mily asked that they sit by the fireplace, she enjoyed so much, to eat their second helpings. They relaxed as they shared and laughed about all the week's events and the seriousness of life and how quickly it can all change.

Emily drew a big breath after she'd eaten her cake and sipped some tea. She looked at each one and smiled. "When I went to bed last night, I realized I didn't want to miss any of you, it broke my heart just thinking about it. When I got up this morning it seemed clear to me what my decision should be. You told me, Betsy, I'm the only one who knows what will make me happy." Emily looked at Betsy with teary eyes. "The desire of my heart is to be loved. I don't need expensive gifts; I need someone's love. My sister, Sally, told me not to do what's expected of me, but do what makes me happy. This week proved to me that Cooper didn't make me happy. I saw a side of him I didn't like, it was deception and manipulation, not true and lasting love. What I saw and felt here made me happy, more than I dreamed possible. You showed me what caring means," she said as a tear slowly crept down her cheek. "These are good tears," she said, as she wiped them away. Emily grinned and continued, "I want to move to Parsons and become part of this community, part of this mountain family." Betsy gasped and clapped her hands. Ben smiled big and Andy gave her a crooked grin.

"So, I guess I'm asking for your help to make this happen," Emily said, with a questioning expression.

"Nothing would make me happier, Em, than to help you move here and you're welcome to live here, in our home, as long as you'd like. We'll get it figured out after the new year. And I'm thrilled you'll be here so I can teach you in person how to cook, instead of sending you recipes." Betsy giggled and hugged Emily.

"I just would never have guessed you'd want to live in this three church-two stoplights-one lawyer kind of town."

Ben grinned at Emily. "But I just happen to know someone that needs to talk to you, Emily." Ben looked at Betsy as his eyes twinkled. "He's in dire need of a paralegal's assistance. And he'll pay top dollar and I'll see to it myself." Ben chuckled and nodded his head as Emily looked stunned.

Emily's eyes then turned to Andy and she gave him a sweet smile. "And my heart has felt more for you, Andy, in a week's time than I've ever felt for anyone. I don't know where this might go but I think the journey might be interesting." Emily's cheeks flushed as she gazed down.

Andy stood and pulled Emily up from the chair and hugged her, as he stroked her hair. She felt the same gentleness of his touch, as she had when he lifted her from the wrecked car and brought her in from a cold, dark night. She heard his heartbeat, steady and strong, as she lay her head on his chest. He pulled her back to look into her eyes, and as he did, the bell rang loud and clear, in angelic harmony for several seconds and then grew quiet.

"That's a lovely bell," Ben said, and was the only one who commented. Andy and Emily only heard the song of their new love. But Betsy smiled—a satisfied expression on her face.

s the cinnamon rolls baked in the oven, the house was filled with laughter, merriment, and joy. Each person contributed their own, to the stories and humor, as they waited for the sweet delights of the delectable bread and enjoyed the hominess of Betsy's B&B. This was, after all, the things that had happened to lead up to Christmas morning on Glimmer Mountain.

"Merry Christmas everyone," Emily said exuberantly, as she held up her cinnamon roll. Betsy, Ben and Andy all tapped their rolls against hers, smiling, and returned the wish, before their first bites. It pleased Emily that she had started and passed along a tradition of her own.

"Andy, have you had a chance yet to speak to your mom about my offer?" Ben said, before he took another bite.

"Well, Sheriff Murphy, I've been just a tad busy and it totally slipped my mind." Andy chuckled and looked at his mom. Betsy seemed puzzled by their cryptic exchange.

"Mom, the sheriff here has asked me to be his deputy. I told him it would be entirely up to you because I promised you, I'd never have another job that put me in harm's way. If you don't want me in that position, I would totally understand, honestly, Mom," Andy said, with sincerity in his voice and respect written on his face.

Betsy's expression was pensive as she appeared to be thinking. She looked at Ben and leaned forward, put her elbows on the table and rested her chin on her folded hands. "Tell me, Ben, why do you need a deputy now?" She smiled and looked ready to scrutinize his answer.

"I don't fool you a bit—do I, Betsy?" Ben grinned at her and she grinned back. "So, I plan to retire in a couple years, and I need someone ready to step into that job."

"And just what do you plan to do with all your newfound free time, Ben Murphy?" Betsy looked like a cat that cornered a mouse, all she needed was a tail to swish.

Ben laughed out loud and slapped the table. "I plan to do a little fishing—and spend a lot more time with you, Betsy Walker. I'd consider myself a lucky man just to have you as my friend for the rest of my life."

"That sounds really good to me, Ben." Betsy's smile widened as she looked at her son.

"Andy, as your mother I probably know you better than you know yourself. I've always known you have a guardian's heart, meant to protect those you love. You have my absolute blessing to accept the sheriff's offer." She reached out and took Andy's hand and he stood to hug her.

"Well, that settles it," Ben said with a grin. "I'll see you in my office on January 11th, Andy, and I'm really looking forward to it."

"Me, too, Ben," Andy said and smiled. "You've been teaching me my whole life, no reason to stop now." The two men hugged and walked in to sit by the fire. They laughed a lot and talked more about the future.

"I'll help with the dishes if you deal with the leftovers, Betsy," Emily said. "That's exciting, I'm so happy for Andy and you're right, he is a guardian." Emily smiled as she remembered how she first met him.

Betsy smiled then giggled. "Andy was so awestruck by you, Em. It seems like ages ago now since he brought you home. But in a private moment after you'd gone to bed, he told me about your first and second meetings. I believe the words he used were 'indescribably beautiful, with long, dark hair, amber eyes you could get lost in, and a delicious sense of humor'," Betsy said. Emily blushed and didn't quite know what to say for a few seconds.

"That's funny because when I crashed into him at the antique store, when he spoke, I suddenly couldn't think of a single thing to say. I just stared at this tall, dark and unbelievably handsome man with amazing, green eyes. Guess what his deep voice reminded me of?" Emily giggled and kept Betsy in suspense.

"Tell me, Em, I'm dying to know now," Betsy pleaded.

Emily gained her composure. "His voice was so deep, and it sounded like—like molasses, thick and sweet." Emily's face froze and then both women laughed until they cried.

*B*etsy excused herself to retrieve her Christmas cards and call Estelle with the good news. She smiled as she walked to the stairs. Emily went into the living room and saw Ben asleep on the couch. Her eyes met Andy's and as she walked past him toward the library, she smiled, and he followed her.

They stopped in front of the large window and quietly absorbed the scenery.

"This is the most beautiful view in the entire world, I think," Emily whispered.

Andy stood close to her and looked down, "Yes—you are, Em."

Andy pulled her close as she put her arms around his waist. He lightly cupped her chin and tilted it up. He stroked her cheek with the back of his fingers, his touch as soft as a butterfly's wings. Her skin was warm and flushed as he grasped her face with both hands, their eyes transfixed. Emily slowly raised her hand and grazed his cheek with her fingertips. They gazed into each other's eyes—and their future. Their lips stopped only a breath away and delayed the inevitable. That sweet, long-awaited kiss was everything—and more. As the bell rang loudly from the Christmas tree, they only heard the beating of their hearts.

The End

Click here to join my newsletter so I can let you know when my next book is coming out.

ACKNOWLEDGMENTS

Loving gratitude to my husband, Joe, for nudging—and challenging—me into realizing my dream of 'one day writing a book'. Without his exceptional skills in all things computer, marketing and e-publishing I would be lost. Without his expertise this book might not exist.

My love and thank you to my daughter, Heather Clifford, for all the years she listened to my incessant book titles, still loved me, and encouraged me to actually write a book. Mahalo!

My love and deepest appreciation to my children, Britt and Heather Clifford, for allowing me to punish them with my puns—their entire lives. You were the first joys in my life.

Thank you to my BFF, Gail Jackson, for all the years we spent listening to and encouraging each other over gallons of iced tea.

Thank you and much appreciation to Judith Shaw for her

excellent editing skills with a 'first book' writer. 'Mahalo nui loa.'

ABOUT THE AUTHOR

My life has led me from the foothills of Northern California, to Interior Alaska, the beaches of Kona, Hawaii and finally the high desert of Arizona. Along the way I've been a mom, wife, bookkeeper, camp cook at a gold mining operation, lay counselor, singer, entrepreneur, photographer and friend. I've tried to live a life of compassion, empathy and humor. I've done much more listening than speaking. (My children may disagree!)

Besides a story meant to entertain, it is my desire for you to glean hope, inspiration and encouragement from these words. Wherever you are in life, it is my wish that you walk among angels unaware.

"May you laugh till it hurts... and love till it doesn't."

--Eila Trent

CPSIA information can be obtained
at www.ICGtesting.com
Printed in the USA
LVHW031944150222
711192LV00003B/181

9 781953 065049